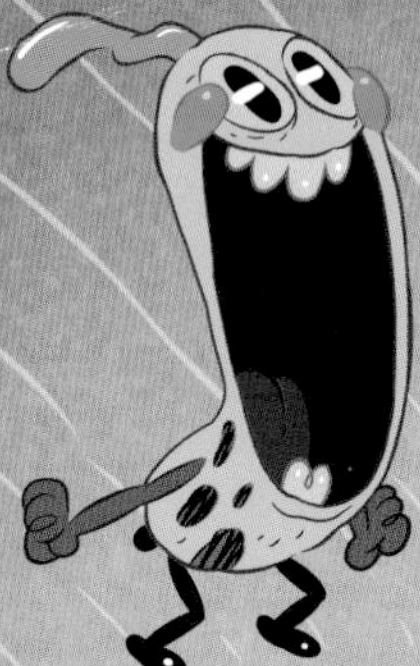

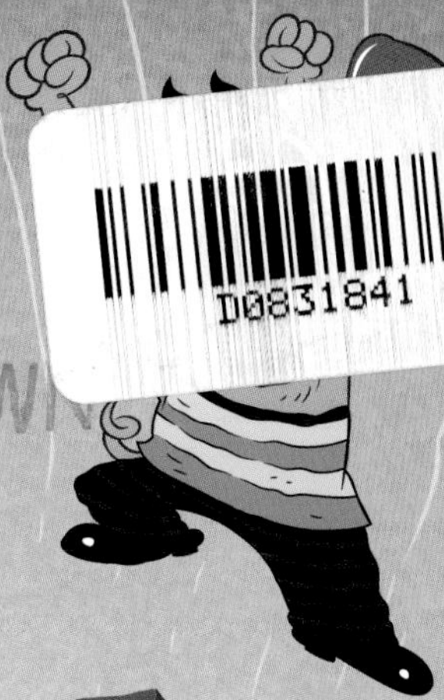

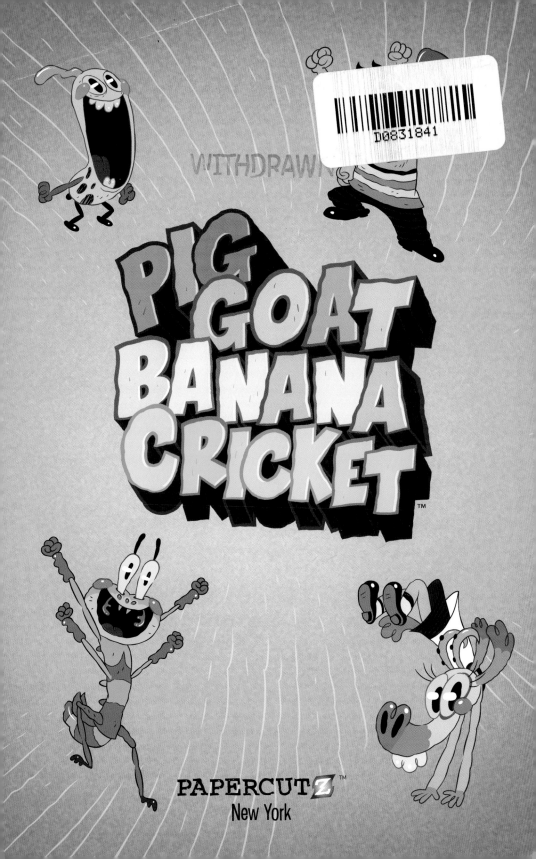

PIG GOAT BANANA CRICKET™

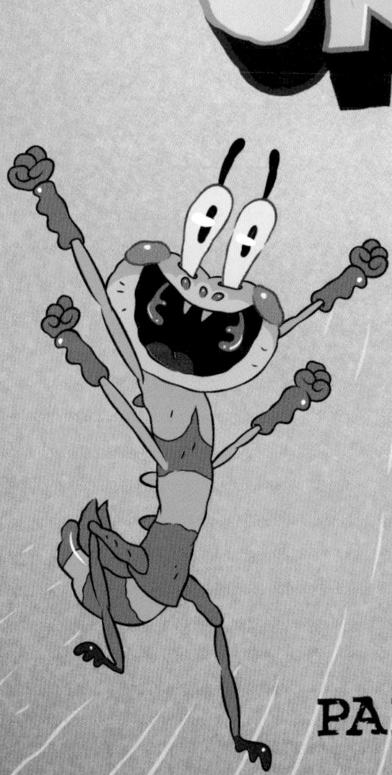

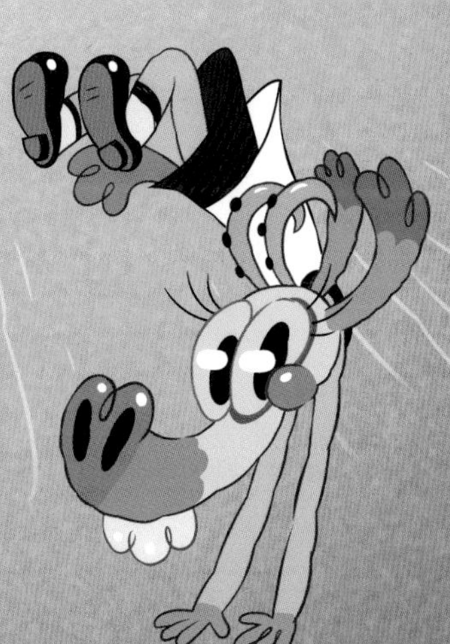

PAPERCUTZ™
New York

nickelodeon GRAPHIC NOVELS AVAILABLE FROM PAPERCUTZ

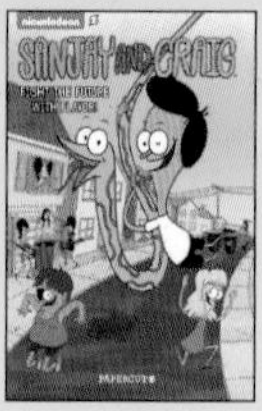
#1 "Fight the Future with Flavor"

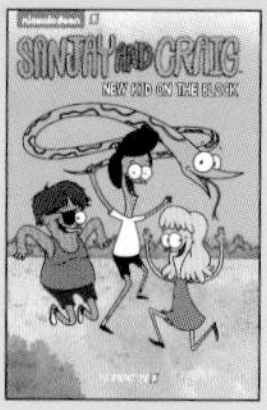
#2 "New Kid on the Block"

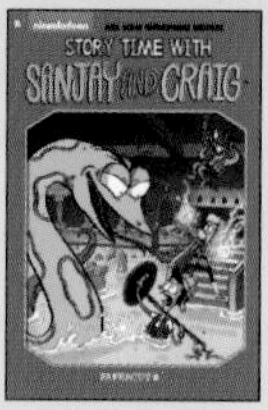
#3 "Story Time with Sanjay and Craig"

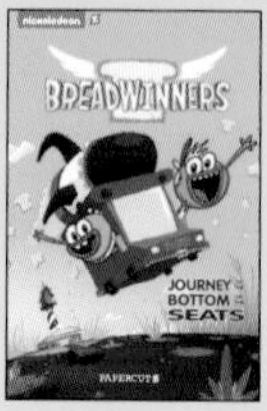
#1 "Journey to the Bottom of the Seats"

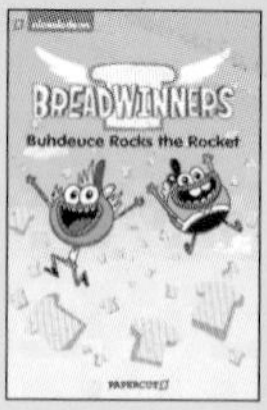
#2 "Buhdeuce Rock the Rocket"

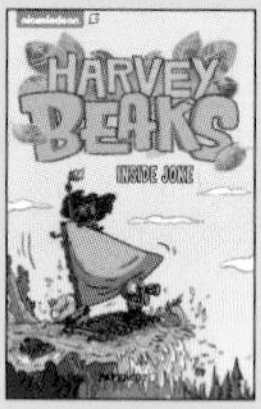
#1 "Inside Joke"

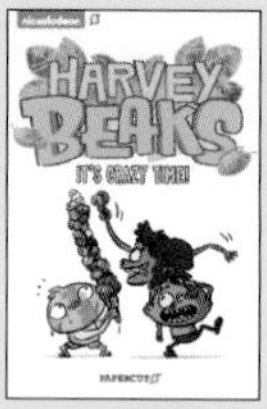
#2 "It's Crazy Time"

COMING SOON!

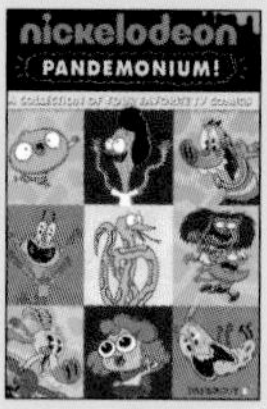
#1 Nickelodeon Pandemonium

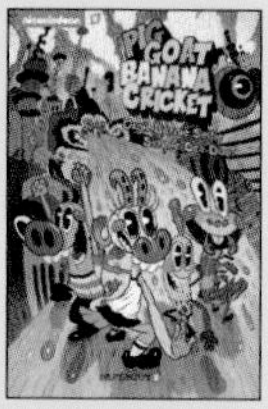
#1 "Orgle Borgle Selfie Simple-Dee-Doo!"

COMING SOON

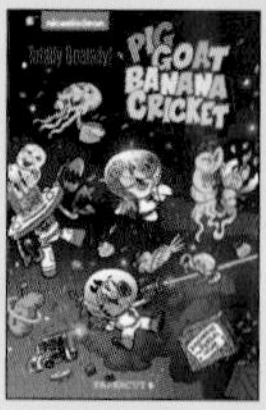
#2 "Totally Goatally

Nickelodeon graphic novels are available for $7.99 in paperback, $12.99 in hardcover. Available from booksellers everywhere. You can also order online from Papercutz.com, or call 1-800-886-1223, Monday through Friday, 9-5 EST. MC, Visa, and AmEx accepted. To order by mail, please add $4.00 for postage and handling for first book ordered, $1.00 for each additional book and make check payable to NBM Publishing. Send to: Papercutz, 160 Broadway, Suite 700, East Wing, New York, NY 10038.

Nickelodeon graphic novels are also available digitally wherever e-books are sold.

SUBSCRIBE!

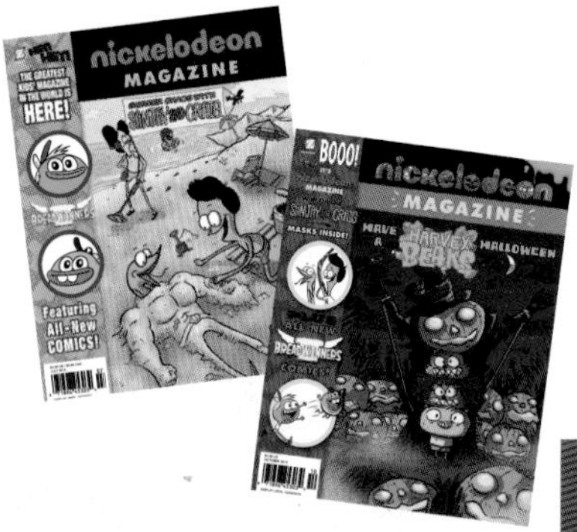

Never miss an issue of

nickelodeon™ MAGAZINE

Get Your Copies Delivered Right to Your Mailbox at Home!

ORDER ONLINE at Papercutz.com/nickmag

OR CALL 1-800-778-6278

(Please have debit/credit card ready)

Use promo code: PGBC1.

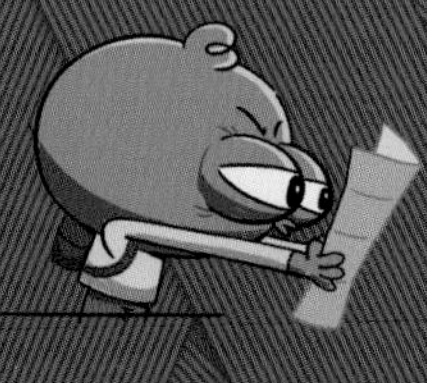

Special Offers

ORDER 6 ISSUES for $25.00 and SAVE $5.00!

ORDER 12 ISSUES for $39.99 and SAVE $20.00!

DIGITAL SUBSCRIPTION: ONLY $19.99 - OR FREE FOR ALL PRINT SUBSCRIBERS!

PIG GOAT BANANA CRICKET™

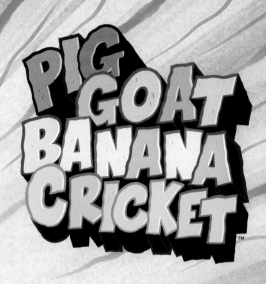

Table of Contents

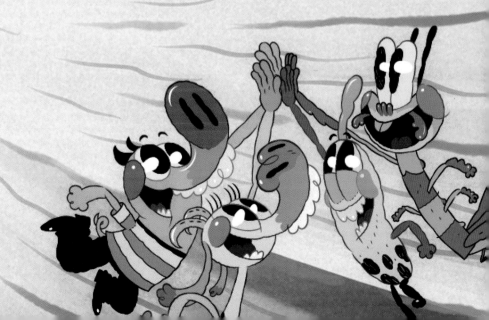

#1 "ORGLE BORGLE SELFIE SIMPLE-DEE-DOO!"

"CRAZY PHOTO SAFARI"
Johnny Ryan and David Sacks – Writers
Brianne Drouhard – Rough Pencils
Dave Cooper – Artist & Letterer
Wes Dzioba – Colorist

"THE BRIDE OF BURGERSTEIN"
Eric Esquivel – Writer
Derek Fridolfs – Artist
Matt Herms – Colorist
Tom Orzechowski – Letterer

"ROTTEN BANANA STRIKES AGAIN""
Eric Esquivel – Writer
Kyle Baker – Artist, Letterer,
and Colorist

"ENTER SANDMAN"
Eric Esquivel – Writer
David DeGrand – Artist
Matt Herms – Colorist
Tom Orzechowski – Letterer

"PICKLEMORPHOSIS"
Eric Esquivel – Writer
David DeGrand – Artist
Matt Herms – Colorist
Tom Orzechowski – Letterer

Based on the Nickelodeon animated TV series created by Johnny Ryan and Dave Cooper.
Dave Cooper – Cover Artist
Bob Camp – Back Cover Artist

James Salerno – Sr. Art Director/Nickelodeon
Chris Nelson – Design/Production
Jeff Whitman – Production Coordinator
Bethany Bryan – Editor
Joan Hilty – Comics Editor/Nickelodeon
Isabella van Ingen – Editorial Intern
Jim Salicrup
Editor-in-Chief

ISBN: 978-1-62991-482-4 paperback edition
ISBN: 978-1-62991-483-1 hardcover edition

Papercutz books may be purchased for business or promotional use. For information on bulk purchases please
contact Macmillan Corporate and Premium Sales Department at (800) 221-7945 x5442.

Printed in Korea
June 2016 through Four Colour Print Group
WE SP Co., Ltd
79-29 Soraji-ro, Paju-Si
Gyeonggi-do, Korea 10863

Distributed by Macmillan
First Printing

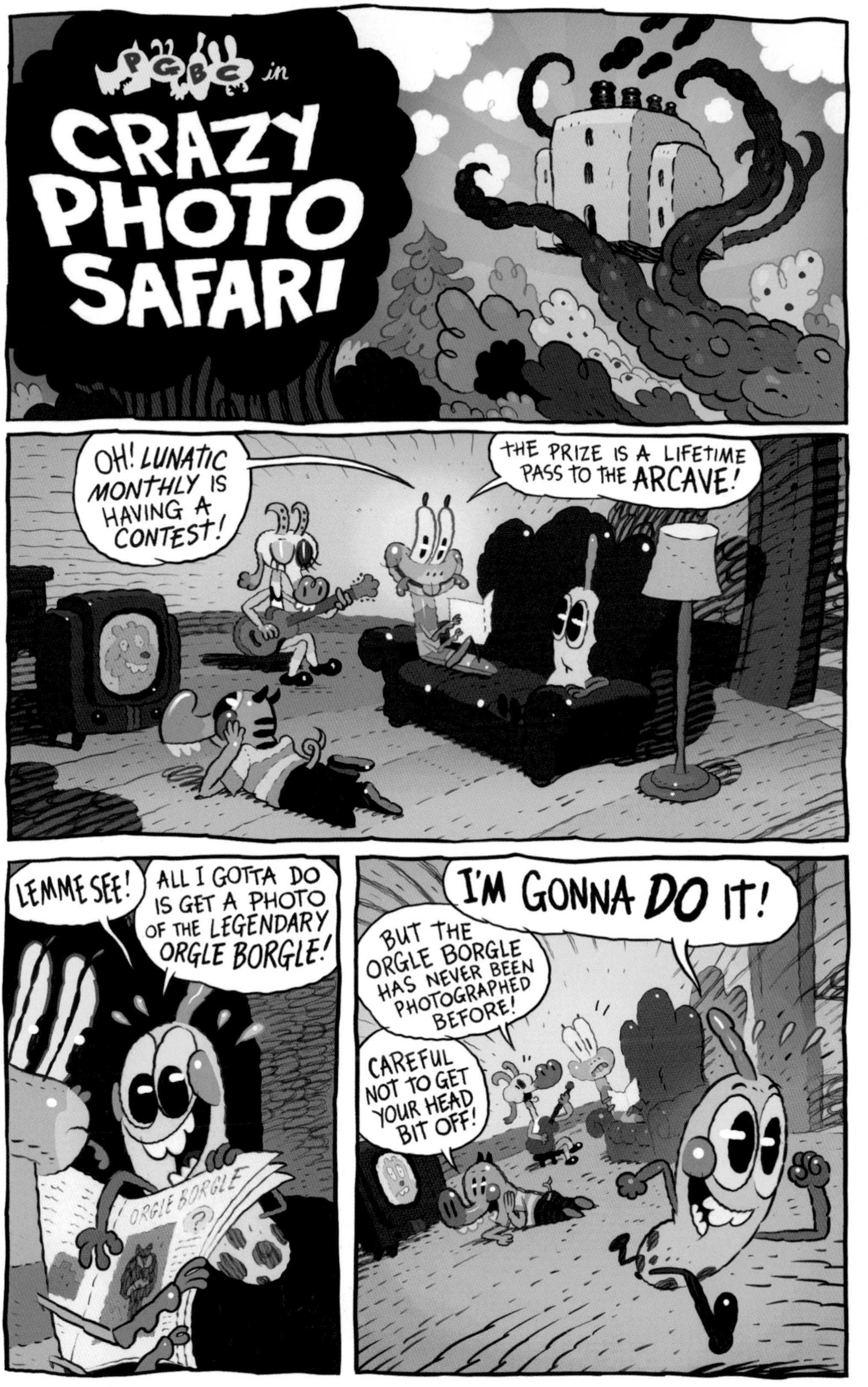
PGBC in
CRAZY PHOTO SAFARI
OH! LUNATIC MONTHLY IS HAVING A CONTEST!
THE PRIZE IS A LIFETIME PASS TO THE ARCAVE!
LEMME SEE!
ALL I GOTTA DO IS GET A PHOTO OF THE LEGENDARY ORGLE BORGLE!
ORGLE BORGLE
I'M GONNA DO IT!
BUT THE ORGLE BORGLE HAS NEVER BEEN PHOTOGRAPHED BEFORE!
CAREFUL NOT TO GET YOUR HEAD BIT OFF!

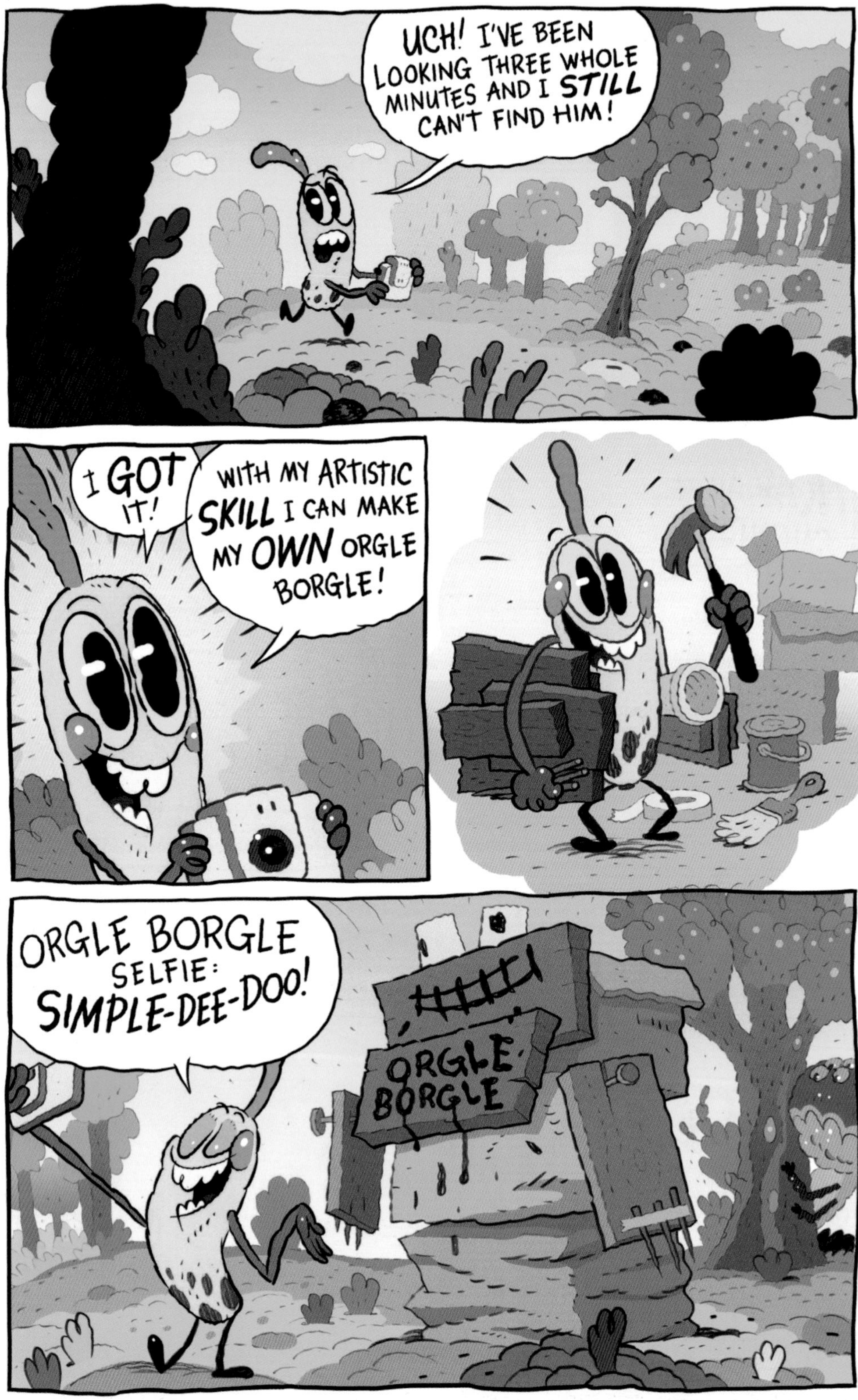
UCH! I'VE BEEN LOOKING THREE WHOLE MINUTES AND I STILL CAN'T FIND HIM!
I GOT IT!
WITH MY ARTISTIC SKILL I CAN MAKE MY OWN ORGLE BORGLE!
ORGLE BORGLE SELFIE: SIMPLE-DEE-DOO!
ORGLE BORGLE

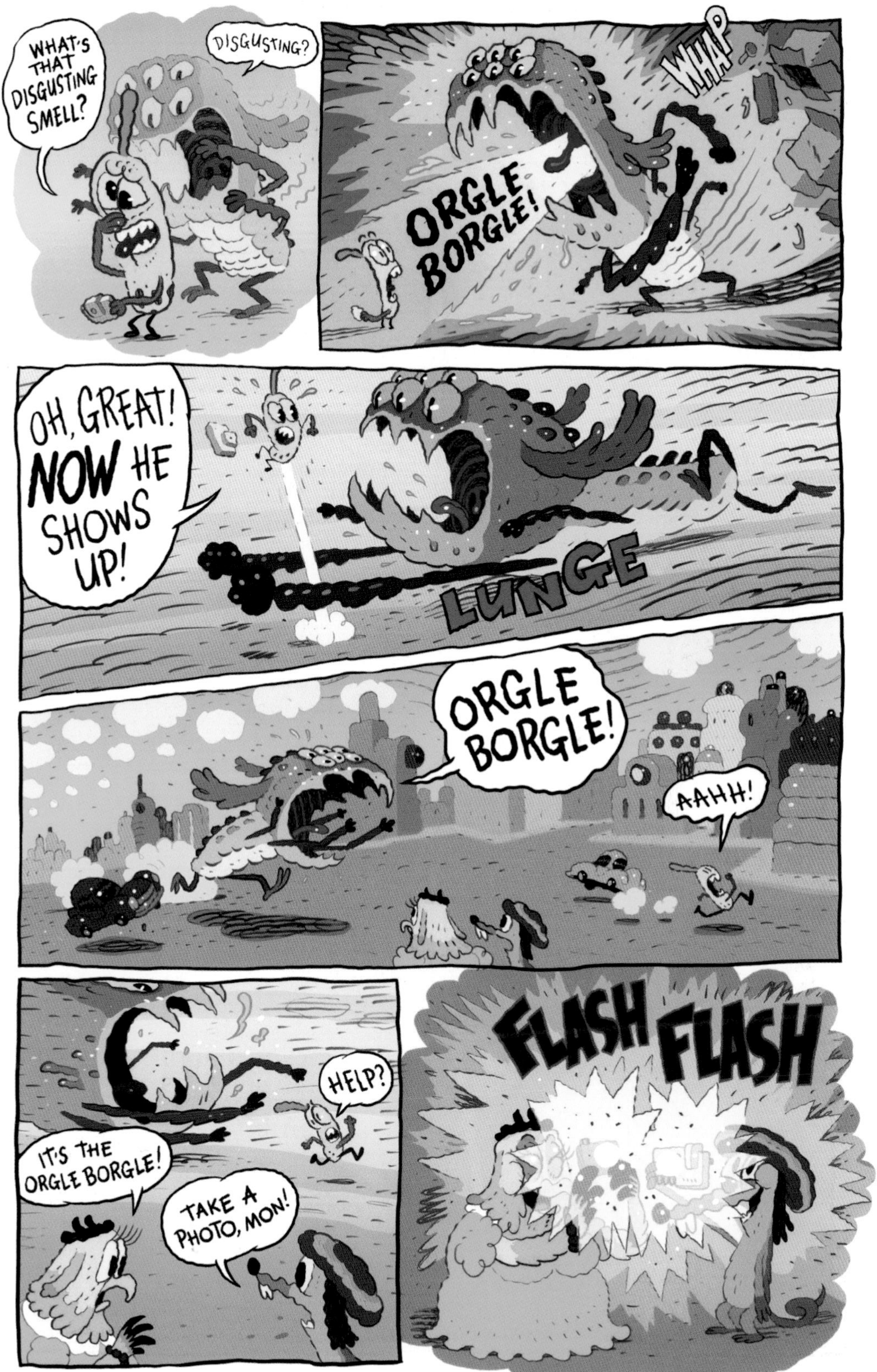
WHAT'S THAT DISGUSTING SMELL?
DISGUSTING?
WHAP
ORGLE BORGLE!
OH, GREAT! NOW HE SHOWS UP!
LUNGE
ORGLE BORGLE!
AAHH!
HELP?
IT'S THE ORGLE BORGLE!
TAKE A PHOTO, MON!
FLASH FLASH

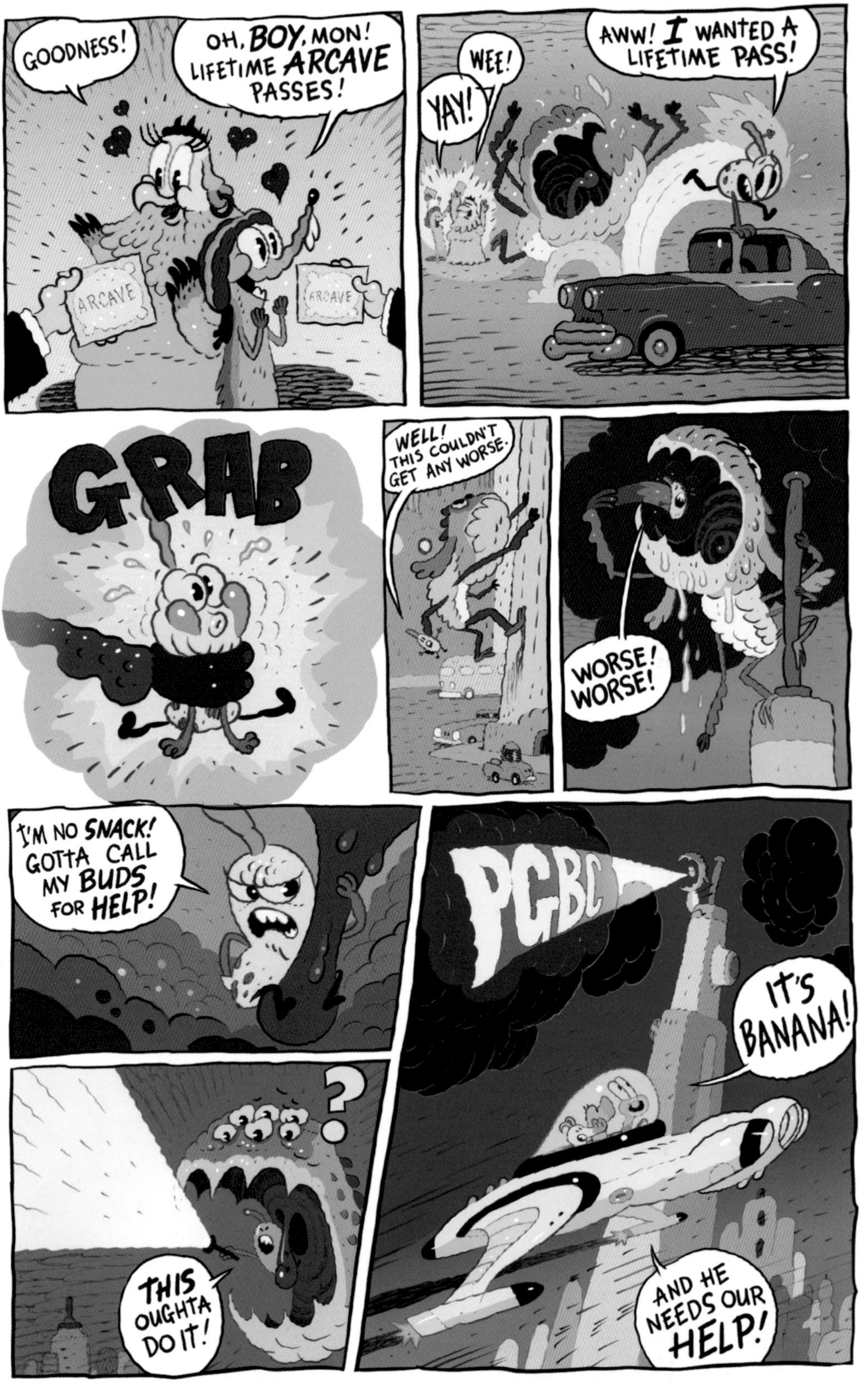
GOODNESS!
OH, BOY, MON! LIFETIME ARCAVE PASSES!
ARCAVE
ARCAVE
YAY!
WEE!
AWW! I WANTED A LIFETIME PASS!
GRAB
WELL! THIS COULDN'T GET ANY WORSE.
WORSE! WORSE!
I'M NO SNACK! GOTTA CALL MY BUDS FOR HELP!
?
THIS OUGHTA DO IT!
PGBC
IT'S BANANA!
AND HE NEEDS OUR HELP!

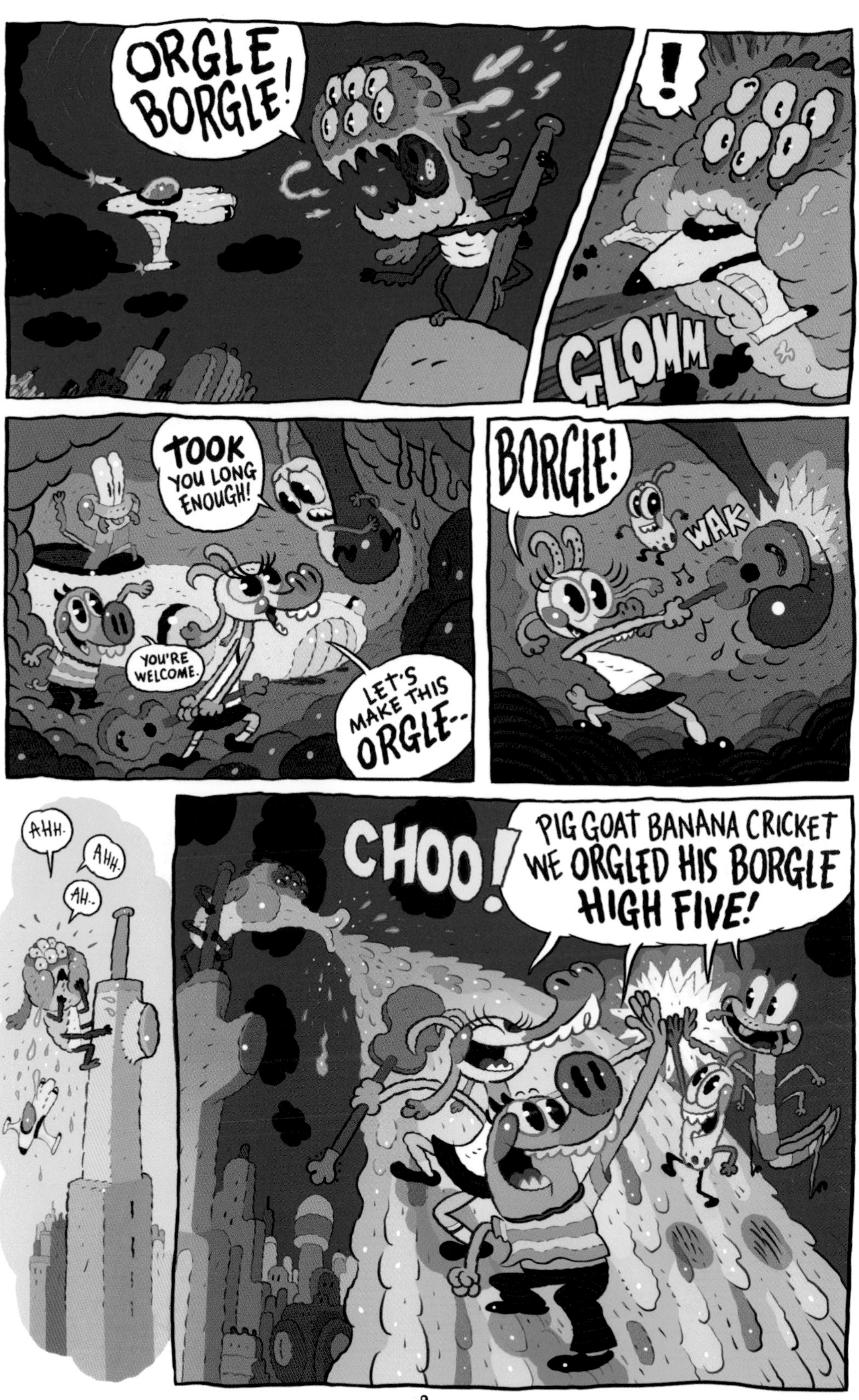
ORGLE BORGLE!
!
GLOMM
TOOK YOU LONG ENOUGH!
YOU'RE WELCOME.
LET'S MAKE THIS ORGLE--
BORGLE!
WAK
AHH-
AHH-
AH--
CHOO!
PIG GOAT BANANA CRICKET WE ORGLED HIS BORGLE HIGH FIVE!

THE END

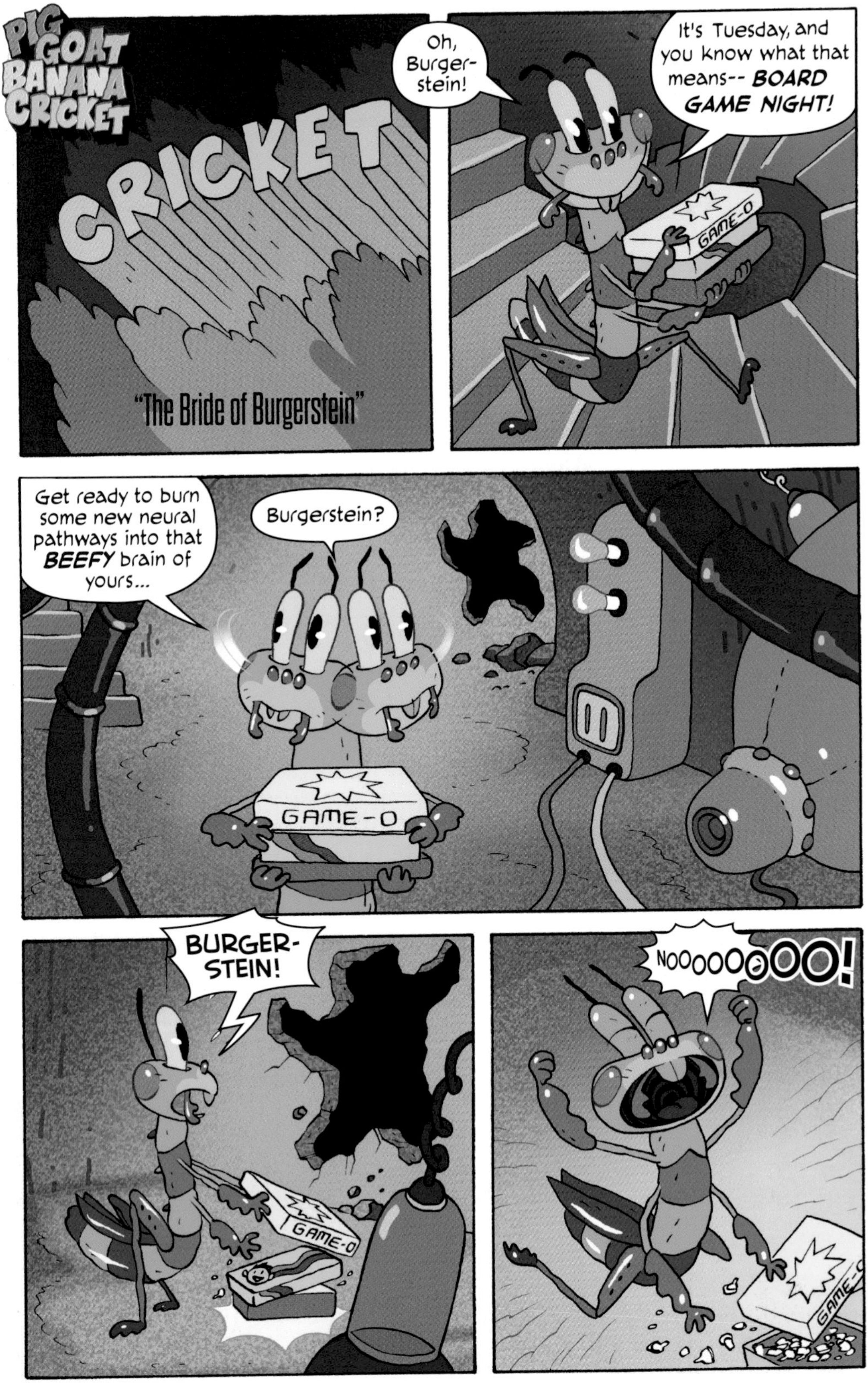
PIG GOAT BANANA CRICKET
CRICKET
"The Bride of Burgerstein"
Oh, Burger-stein!
It's Tuesday, and you know what that means-- BOARD GAME NIGHT!
GAME-O
Get ready to burn some new neural pathways into that BEEFY brain of yours...
Burgerstein?
GAME-O
BURGER-STEIN!
GAME-O
NOOOOOOOO!

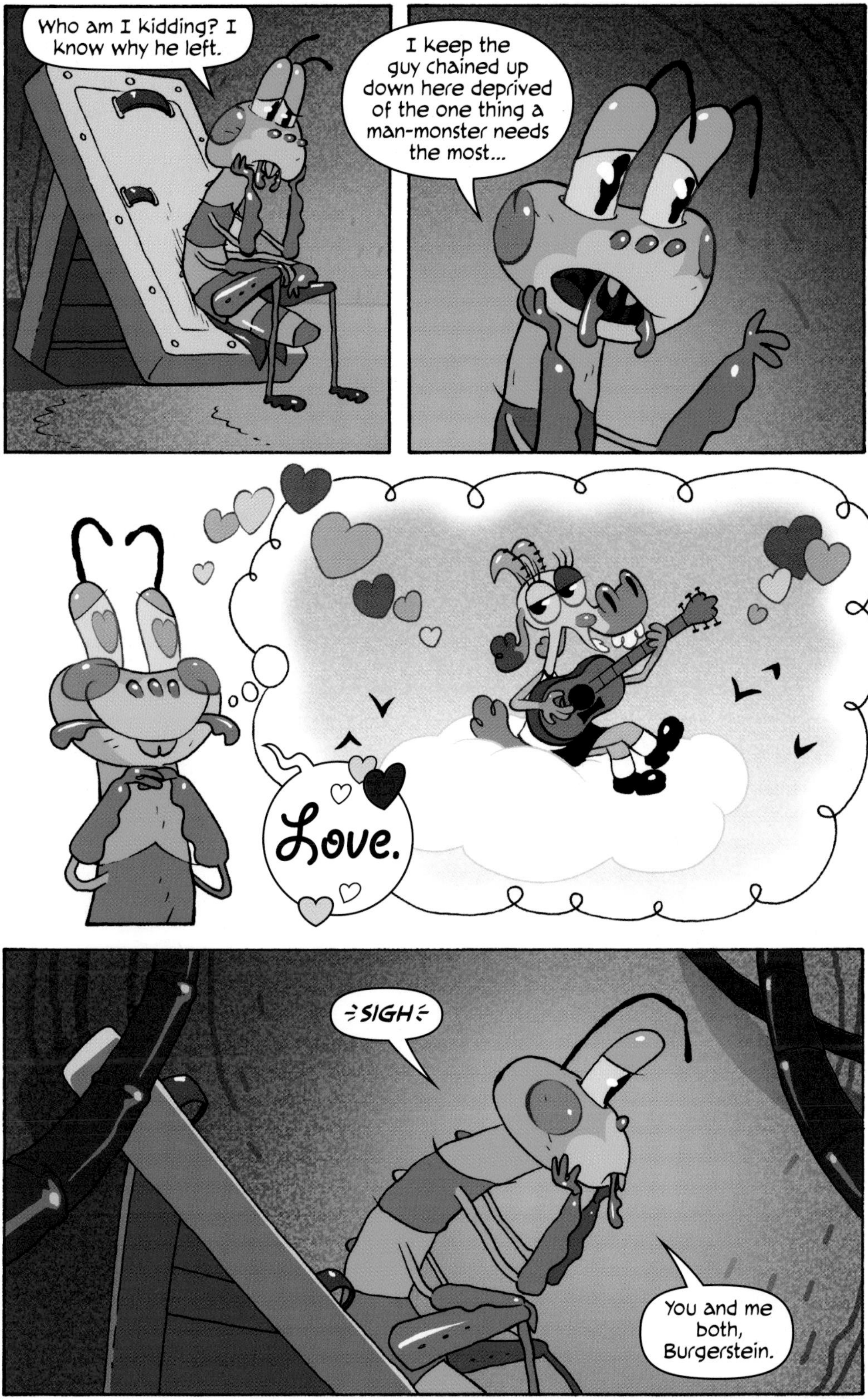
Who am I kidding? I know why he left.
I keep the guy chained up down here deprived of the one thing a man-monster needs the most...
Love.
=SIGH=
You and me both, Burgerstein.

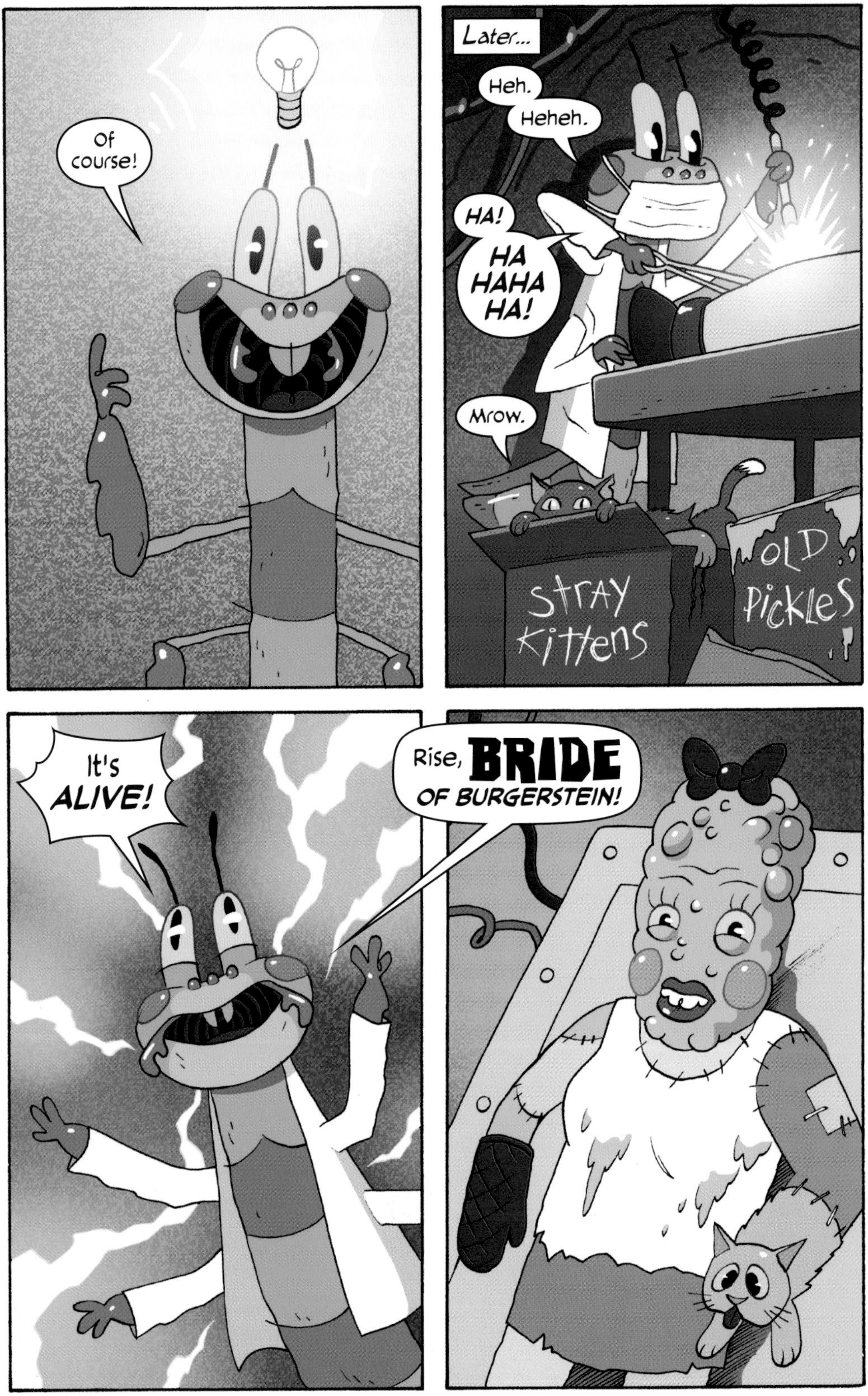
Of course!
Later...
Heh.
Heheh.
HA!
HA HAHA HA!
Mrow.
STRAY KITTENS
OLD PICKLES
It's ALIVE!
Rise, BRIDE OF BURGERSTEIN!

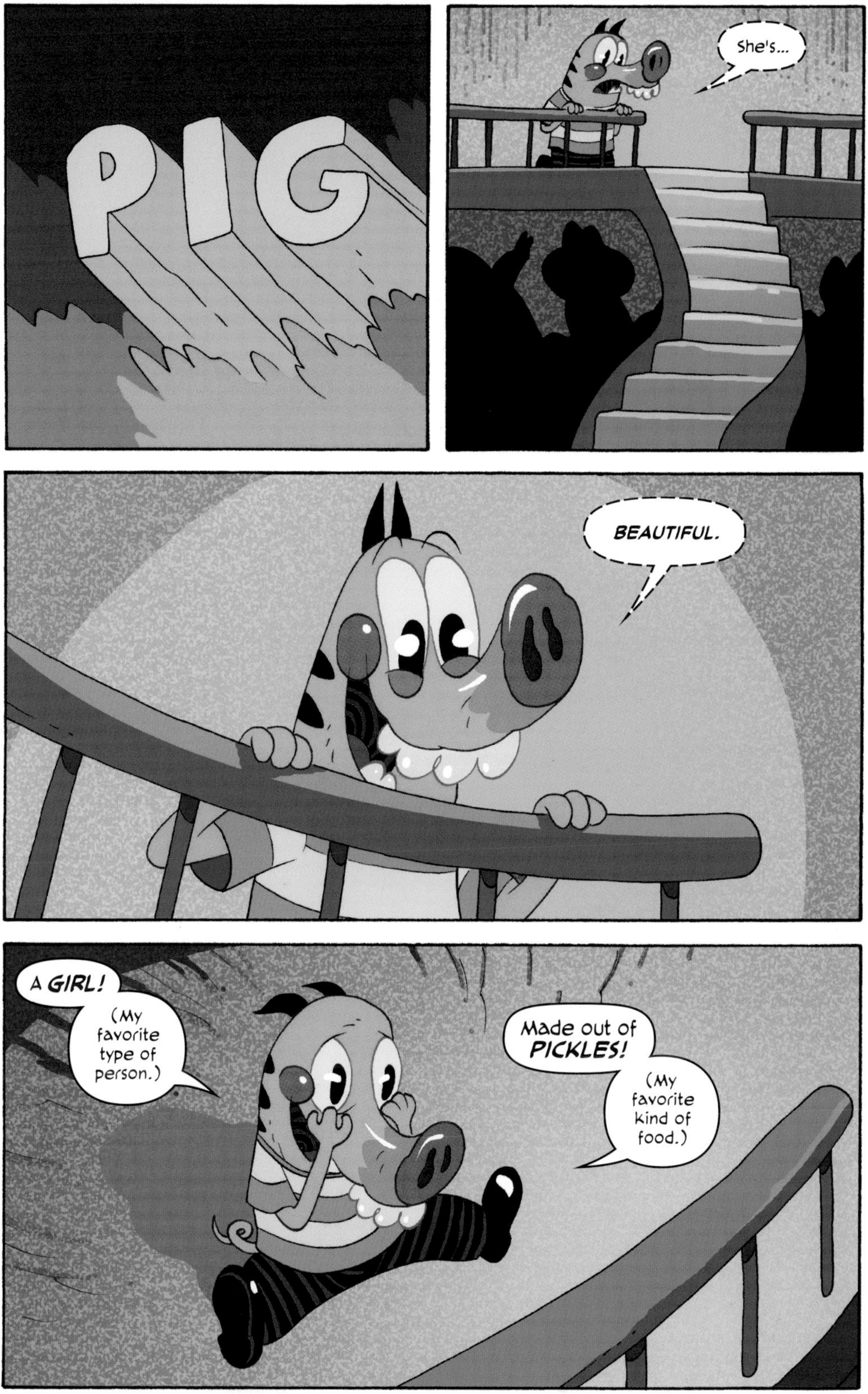
PIG
She's...
BEAUTIFUL.
A GIRL!
(My favorite type of person.)
Made out of PICKLES!
(My favorite kind of food.)

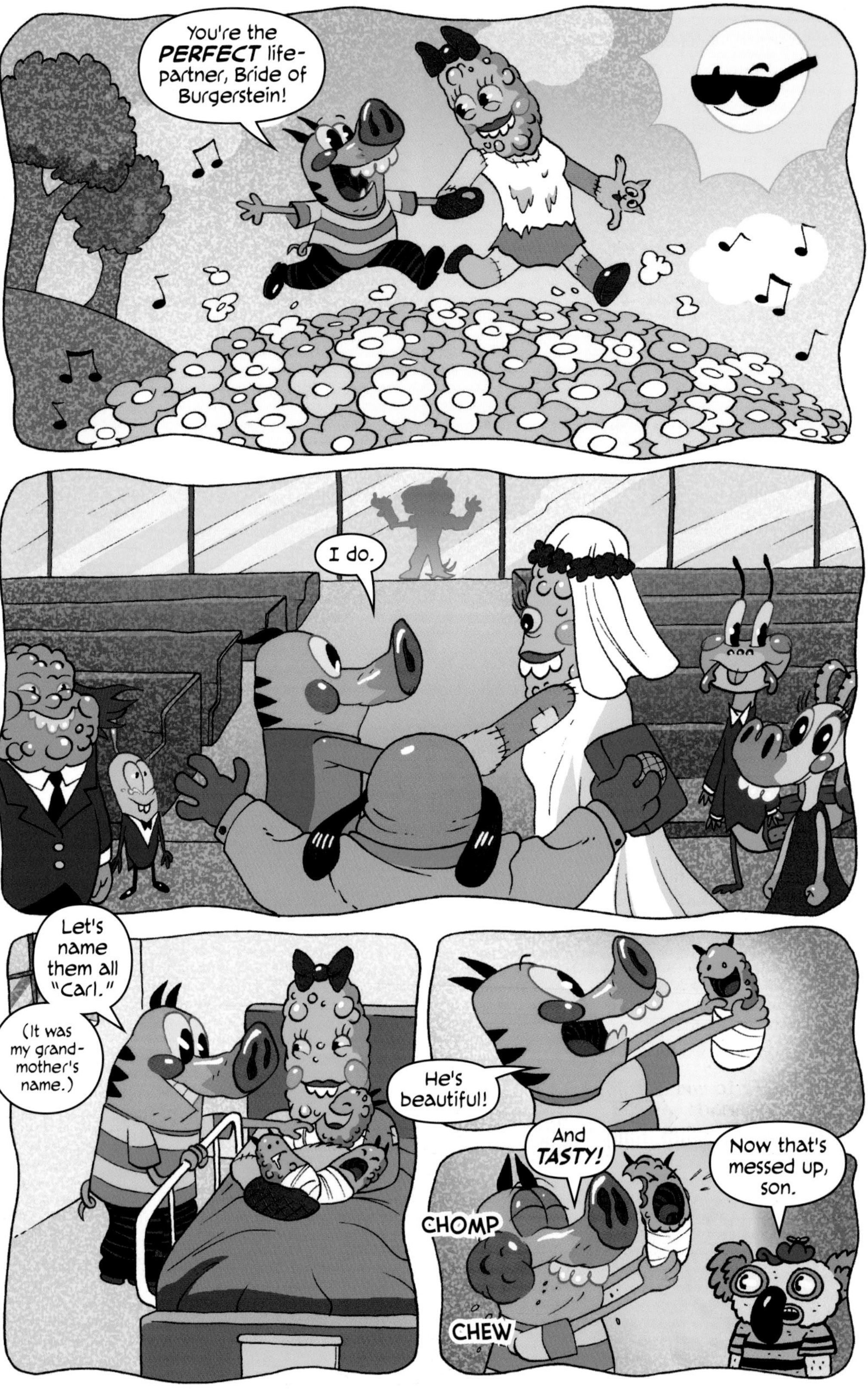
You're the PERFECT life-partner, Bride of Burgerstein!
I do.
Let's name them all "Carl."
(It was my grand-mother's name.)
He's beautiful!
And TASTY!
CHOMP
CHEW
Now that's messed up, son.

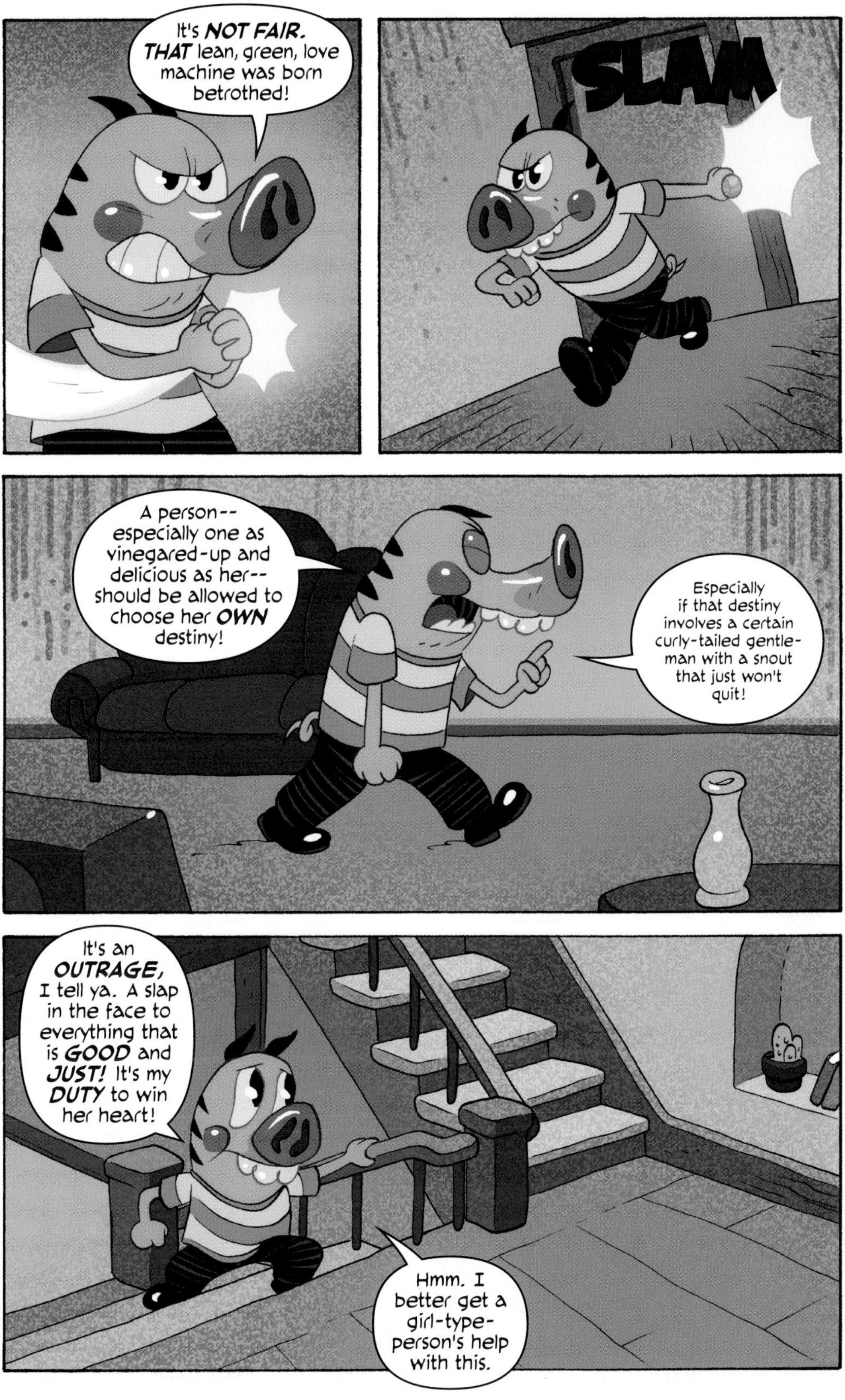

It's NOT FAIR. THAT lean, green, love machine was born betrothed!
SLAM
A person-- especially one as vinegared-up and delicious as her-- should be allowed to choose her OWN destiny!
Especially if that destiny involves a certain curly-tailed gentle-man with a snout that just won't quit!
It's an OUTRAGE, I tell ya. A slap in the face to everything that is GOOD and JUST! It's my DUTY to win her heart!
Hmm. I better get a girl-type-person's help with this.

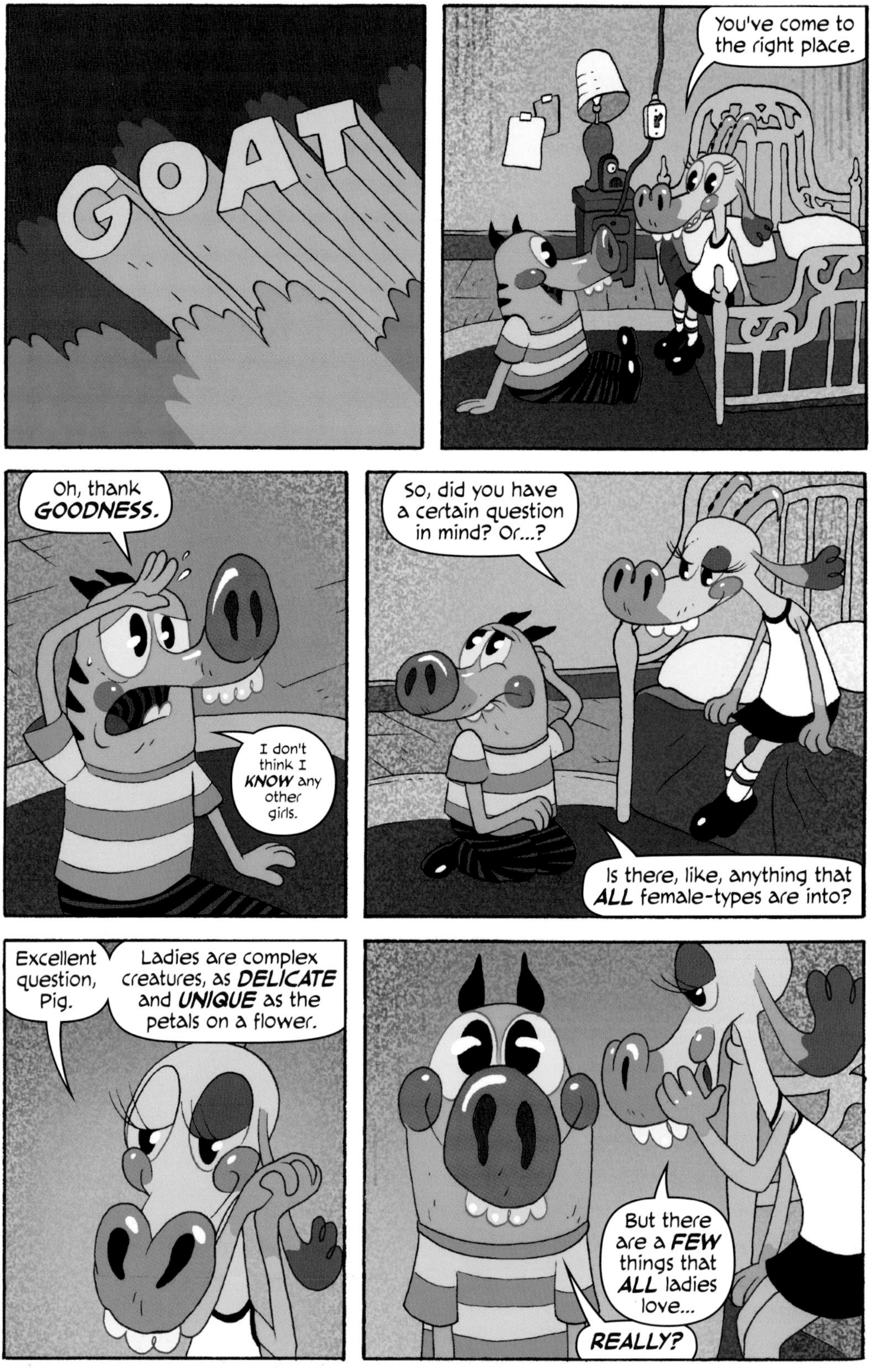
GOAT
You've come to the right place.
Oh, thank GOODNESS.
I don't think I KNOW any other girls.
So, did you have a certain question in mind? Or...?
Is there, like, anything that ALL female-types are into?
Excellent question, Pig.
Ladies are complex creatures, as DELICATE and UNIQUE as the petals on a flower.
But there are a FEW things that ALL ladies love...
REALLY?

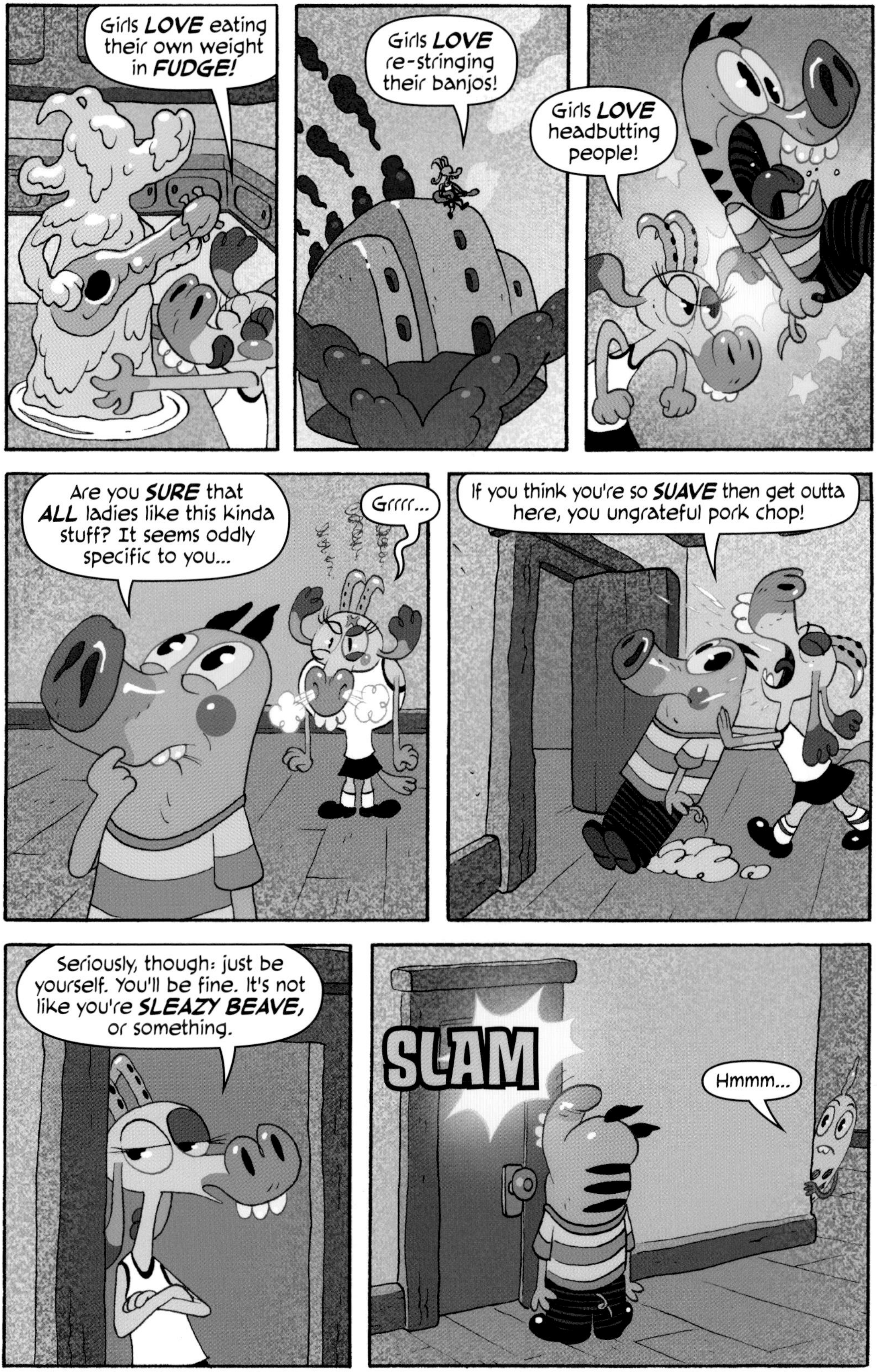
Girls LOVE eating their own weight in FUDGE!
Girls LOVE re-stringing their banjos!
Girls LOVE headbutting people!
Are you SURE that ALL ladies like this kinda stuff? It seems oddly specific to you...
Grrrr...
If you think you're so SUAVE then get outta here, you ungrateful pork chop!
Seriously, though: just be yourself. You'll be fine. It's not like you're SLEAZY BEAVE, or something.
SLAM
Hmmm...

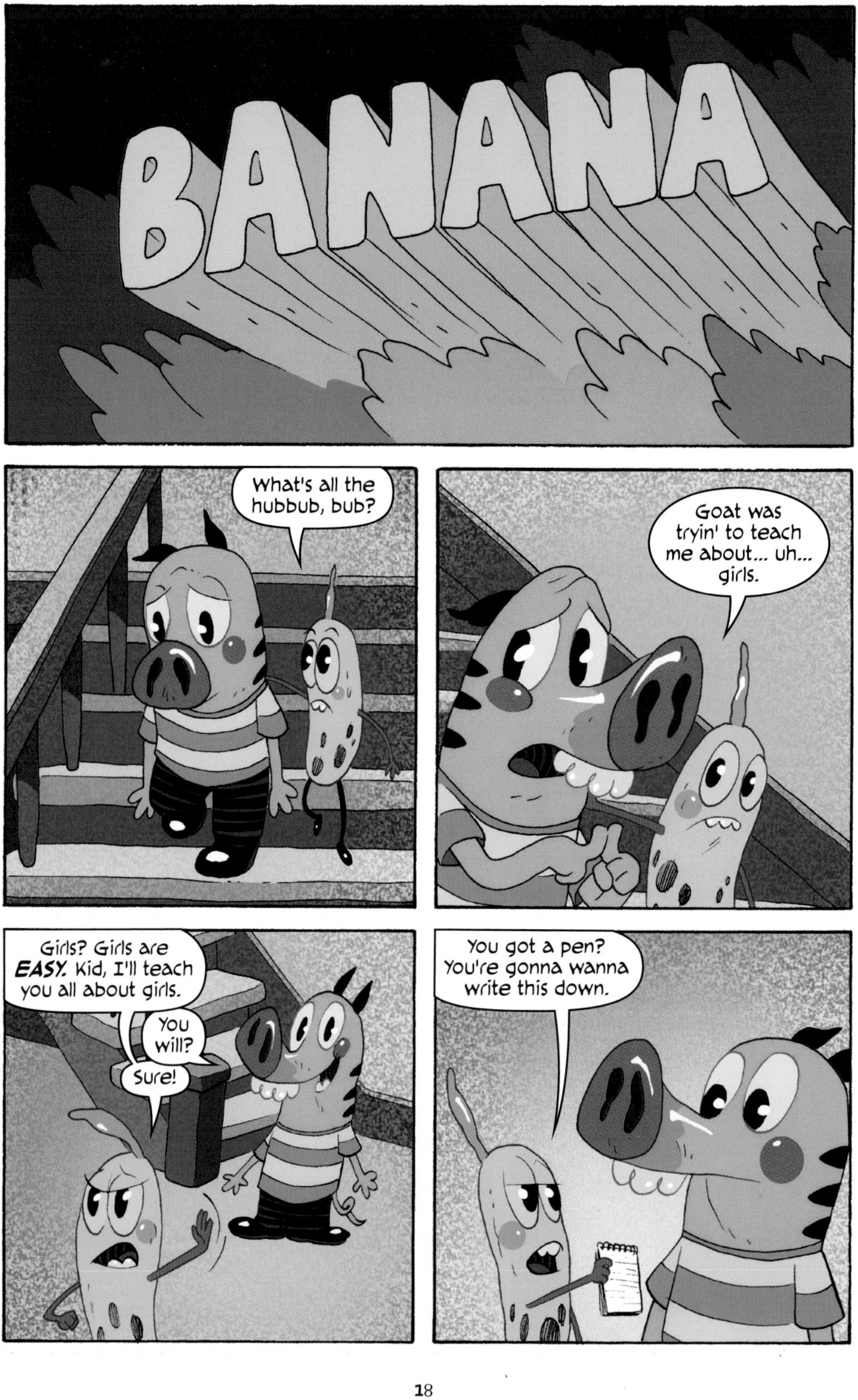
BANANA
What's all the hubbub, bub?
Goat was tryin' to teach me about... uh... girls.
Girls? Girls are EASY. Kid, I'll teach you all about girls.
You will?
Sure!
You got a pen? You're gonna wanna write this down.

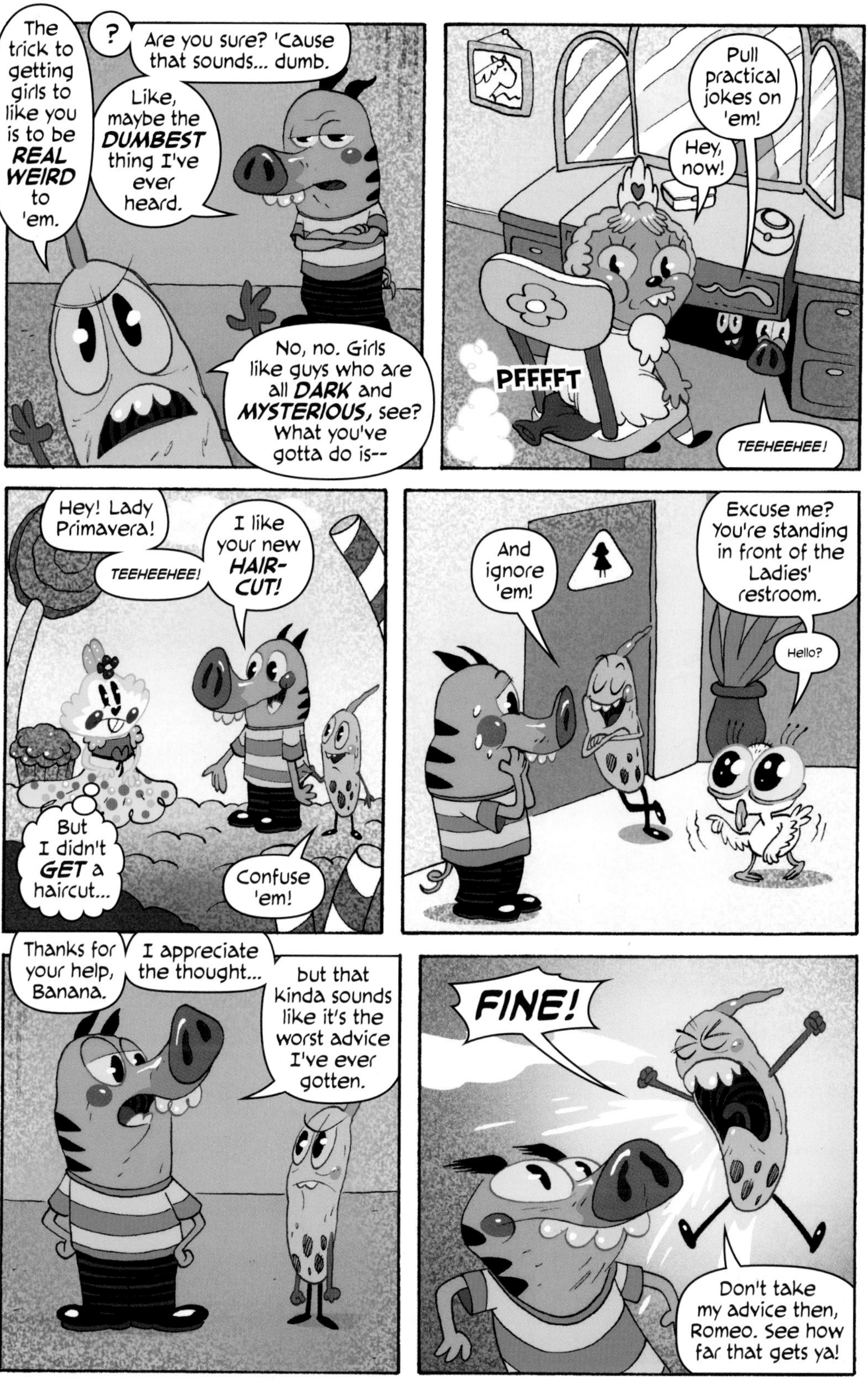
The trick to getting girls to like you is to be REAL WEIRD to 'em.
?
Are you sure? 'Cause that sounds... dumb.
Like, maybe the DUMBEST thing I've ever heard.
No, no. Girls like guys who are all DARK and MYSTERIOUS, see? What you've gotta do is--
Pull practical jokes on 'em!
Hey, now!
PFFFFT
TEEHEEHEE!
Hey! Lady Primavera!
TEEHEEHEE!
I like your new HAIR-CUT!
But I didn't GET a haircut...
Confuse 'em!
And ignore 'em!
Excuse me? You're standing in front of the Ladies' restroom.
Hello?
Thanks for your help, Banana.
I appreciate the thought...
but that kinda sounds like it's the worst advice I've ever gotten.
FINE!
Don't take my advice then, Romeo. See how far that gets ya!

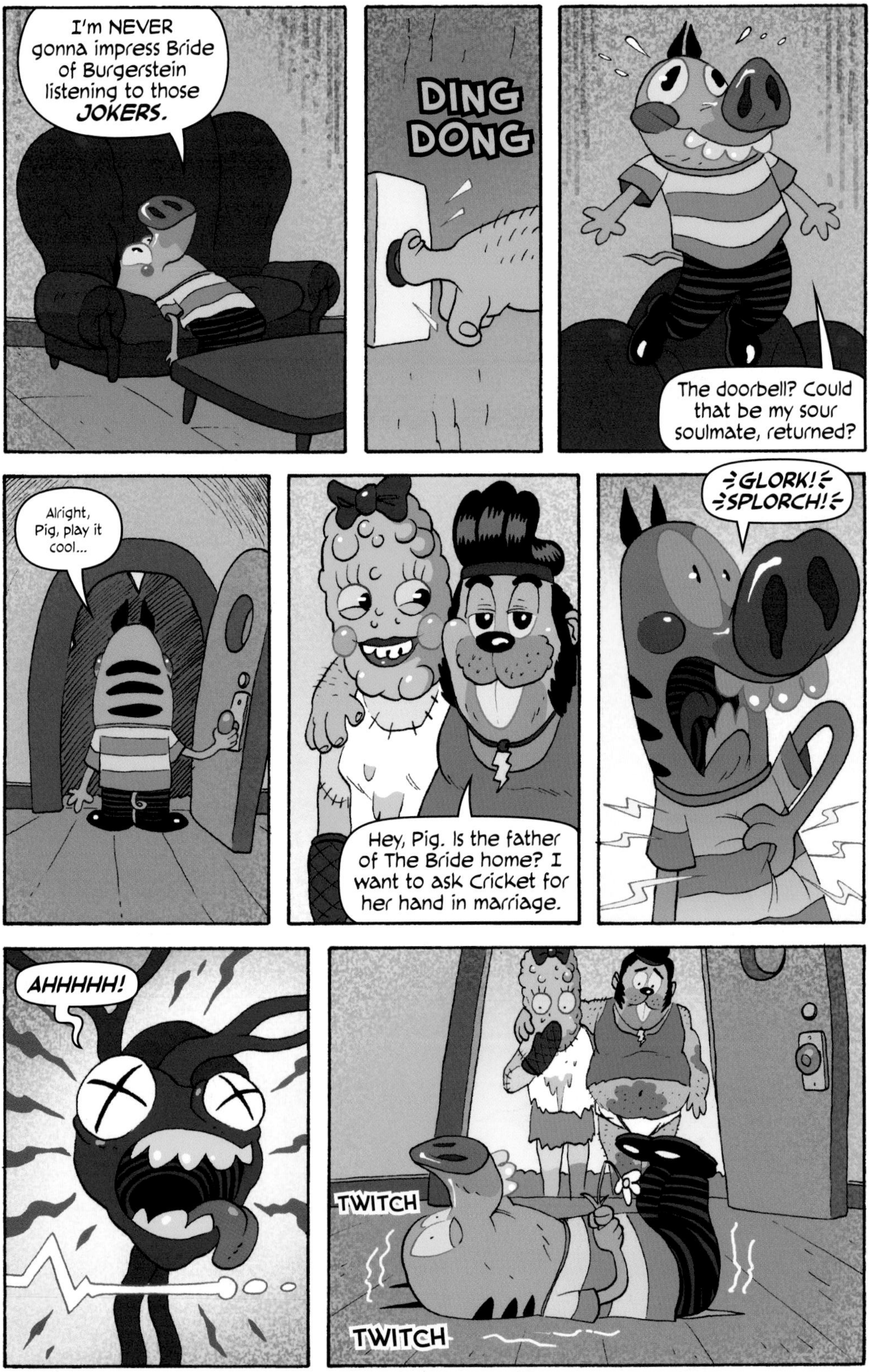
I'm NEVER gonna impress Bride of Burgerstein listening to those JOKERS.
DING DONG
The doorbell? Could that be my sour soulmate, returned?
Alright, Pig, play it cool...
Hey, Pig. Is the father of The Bride home? I want to ask Cricket for her hand in marriage.
GLORK! SPLORCH!
AHHHHH!
TWITCH
TWITCH

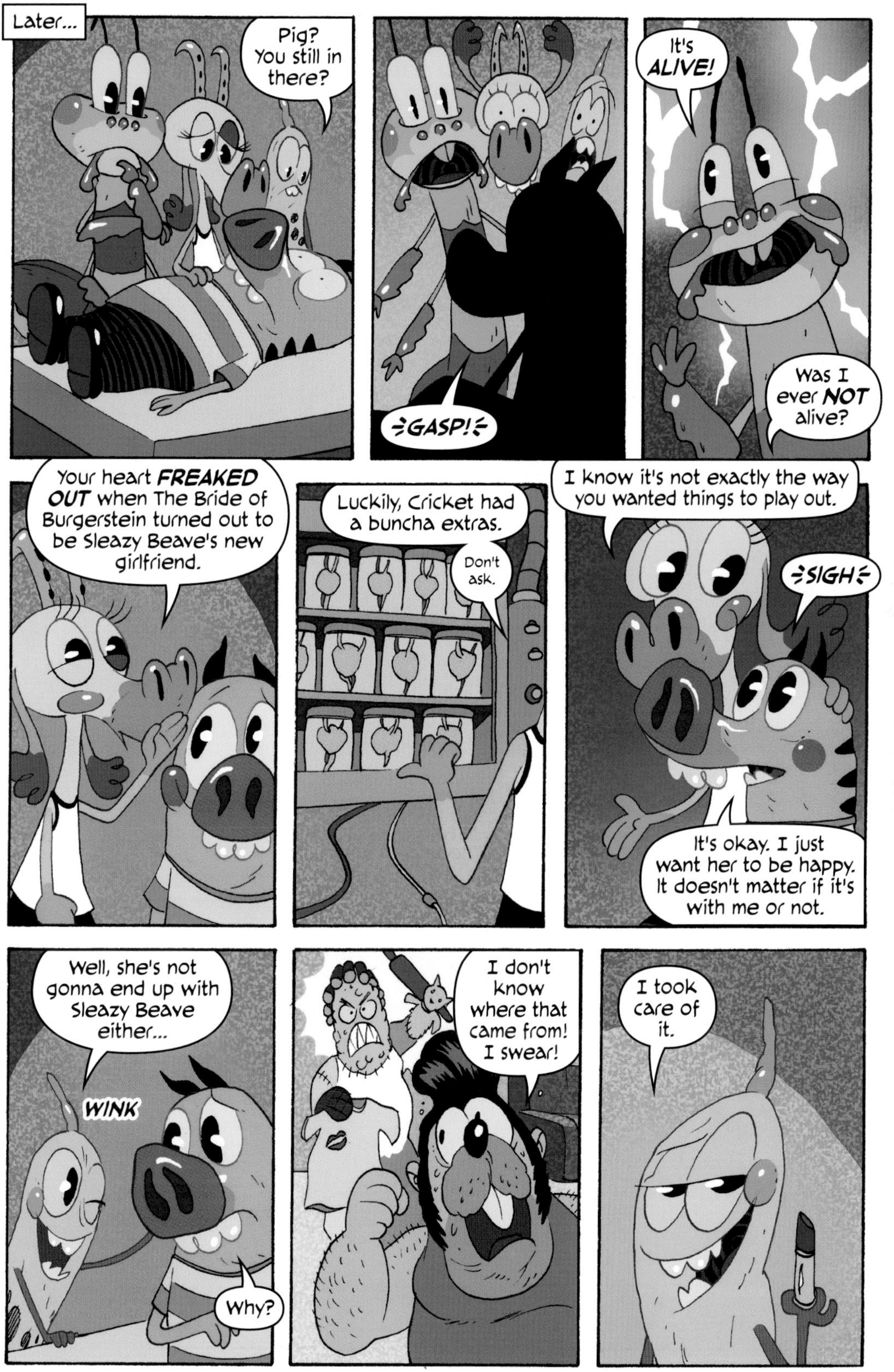

Later...
Pig? You still in there?
GASP!
It's ALIVE!
Was I ever NOT alive?
Your heart FREAKED OUT when The Bride of Burgerstein turned out to be Sleazy Beave's new girlfriend.
Luckily, Cricket had a buncha extras.
Don't ask.
I know it's not exactly the way you wanted things to play out.
SIGH
It's okay. I just want her to be happy. It doesn't matter if it's with me or not.
Well, she's not gonna end up with Sleazy Beave either...
WINK
Why?
I don't know where that came from! I swear!
I took care of it.

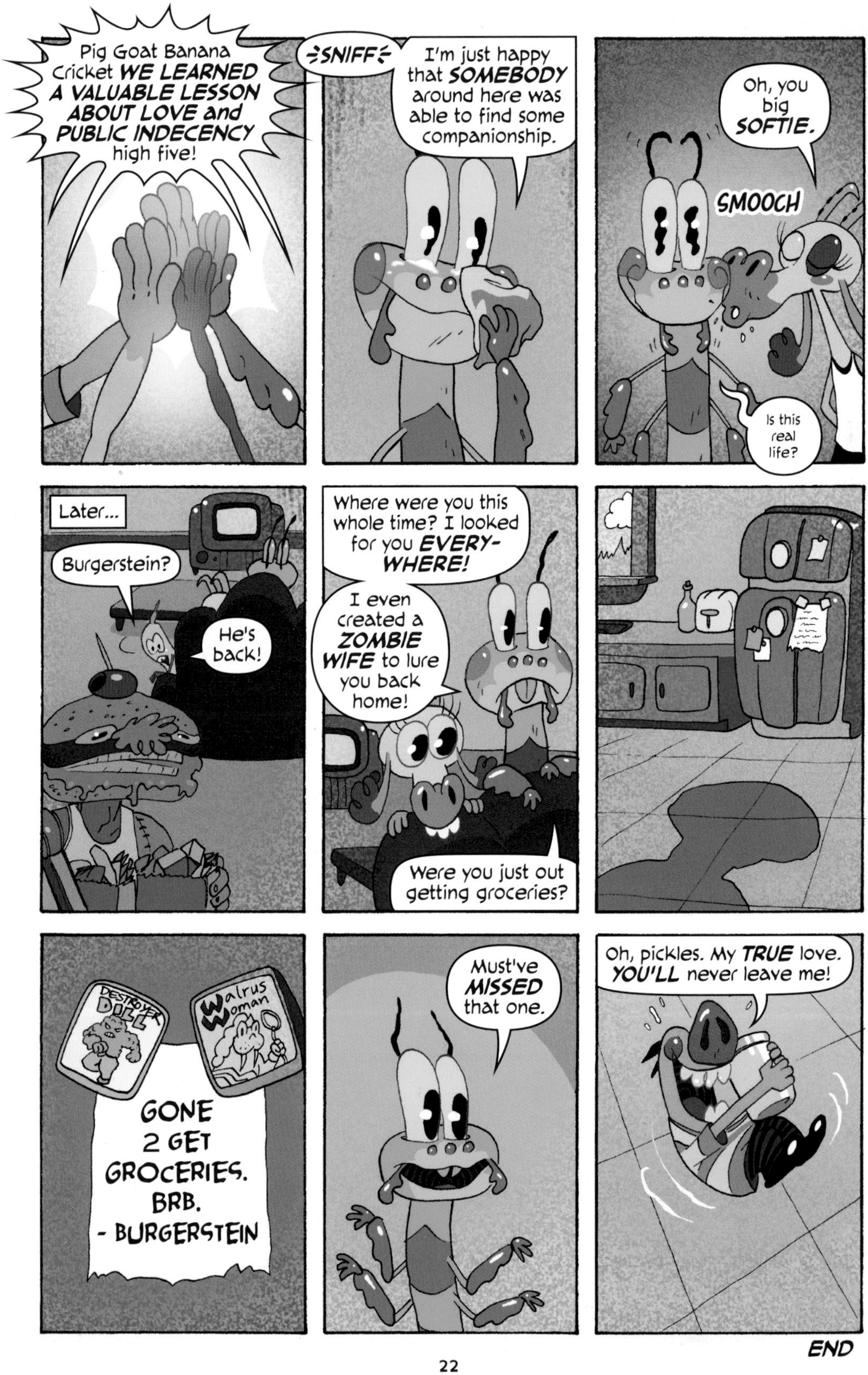
Pig Goat Banana Cricket WE LEARNED A VALUABLE LESSON ABOUT LOVE and PUBLIC INDECENCY high five!
SNIFF
I'm just happy that SOMEBODY around here was able to find some companionship.
Oh, you big SOFTIE.
SMOOCH
Is this real life?
Later...
Burgerstein?
He's back!
Where were you this whole time? I looked for you EVERY-WHERE!
I even created a ZOMBIE WIFE to lure you back home!
Were you just out getting groceries?
DESTROYER DILL
Walrus Woman
GONE 2 GET GROCERIES. BRB. - BURGERSTEIN
Must've MISSED that one.
Oh, pickles. My TRUE love. YOU'LL never leave me!
END

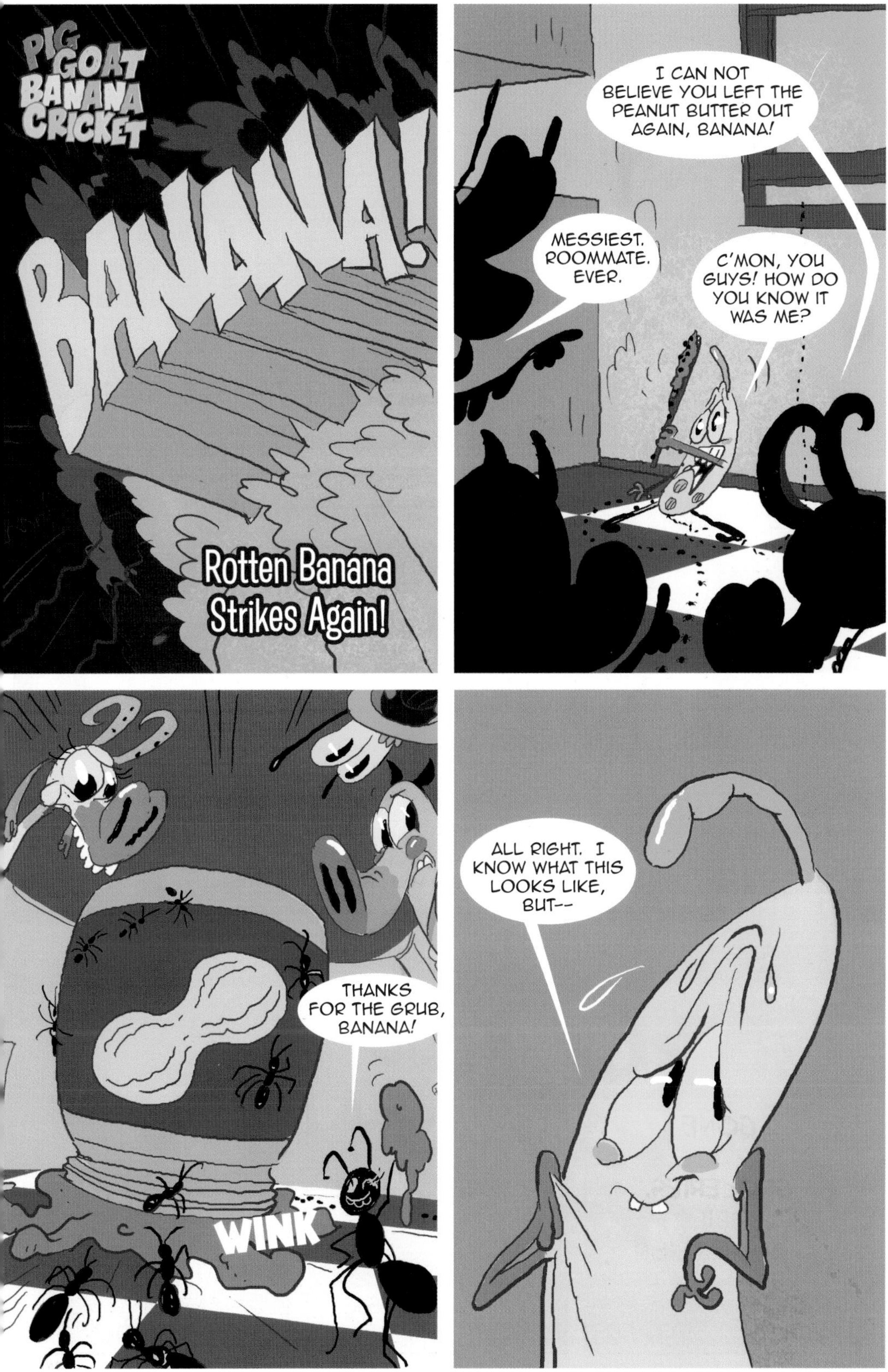
PIG GOAT BANANA CRICKET
BANANA!
Rotten Banana Strikes Again!
I CAN NOT BELIEVE YOU LEFT THE PEANUT BUTTER OUT AGAIN, BANANA!
MESSIEST. ROOMMATE. EVER.
C'MON, YOU GUYS! HOW DO YOU KNOW IT WAS ME?
THANKS FOR THE GRUB, BANANA!
WINK
ALL RIGHT. I KNOW WHAT THIS LOOKS LIKE, BUT--

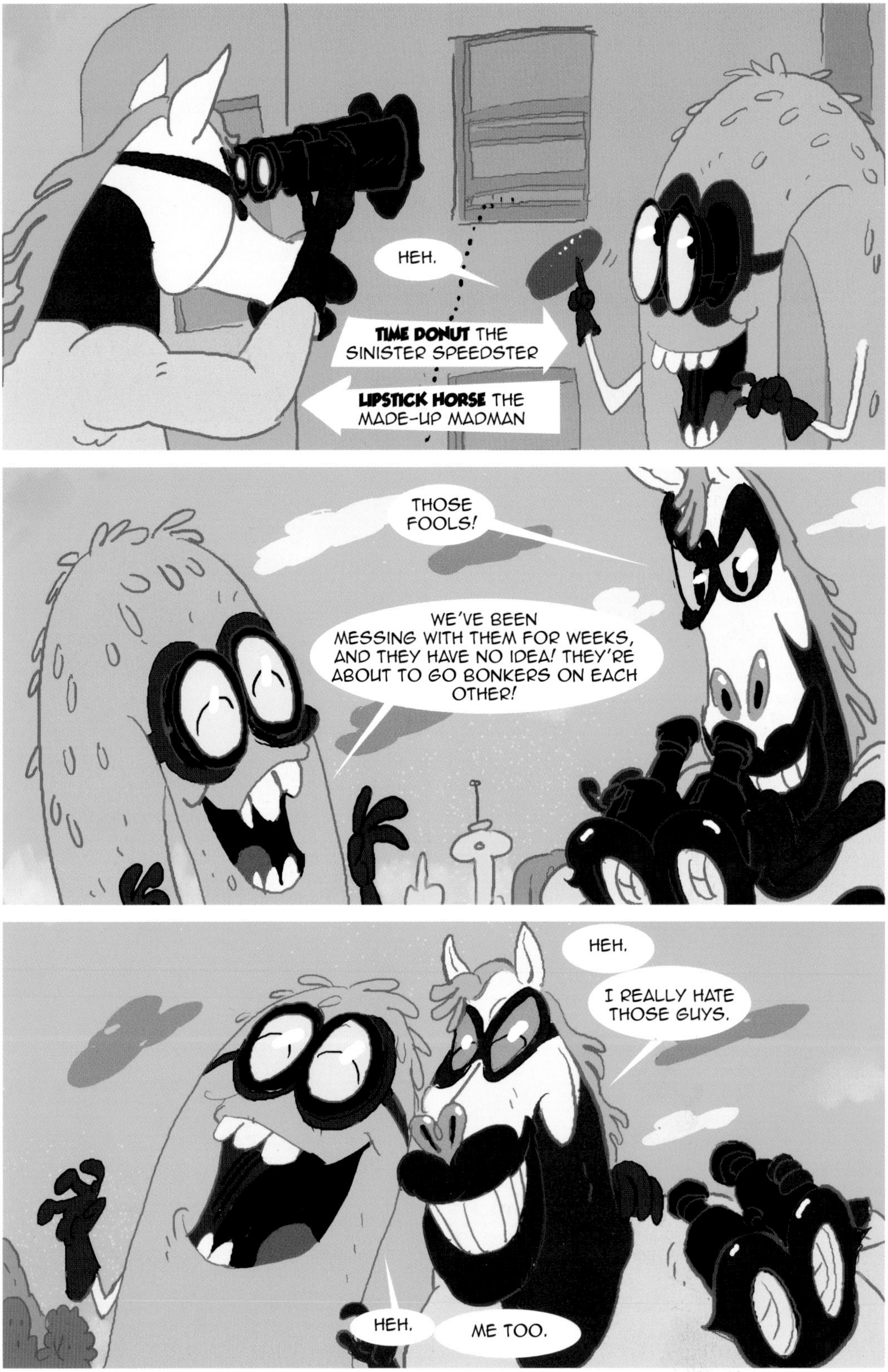
HEH.
TIME DONUT THE SINISTER SPEEDSTER
LIPSTICK HORSE THE MADE-UP MADMAN
THOSE FOOLS!
WE'VE BEEN MESSING WITH THEM FOR WEEKS, AND THEY HAVE NO IDEA! THEY'RE ABOUT TO GO BONKERS ON EACH OTHER!
HEH.
I REALLY HATE THOSE GUYS.
HEH.
ME TOO.

"I, LIPSTICK HORSE, WILL NEVER FORGIVE THOSE DO-GOODERS FOR THWARTING OUR EVIL PLANS!"*

"IT WASN'T ALL BAD, THOUGH. REMEMBER WHEN WE TRICKED BANANA INTO PUTTING ON THAT EVIL COSTUME AND TURNING INTO THE *ROTTEN BANANA*?"

"YEAH! THAT WAS THE WORST WEDNESDAY I, TIME DONUT, EVER HAD!"

*THE SUPER SPACE MEATBALL EPISODE

I MISS THAT DEVILISHLY DECAYED LITTLE FRUIT. HE WAS SO GOOD WHEN HE WAS BAD.

ME TOO! OUR TERRIBLE TRIO JUST ISN'T THE SAME WITH TWO.

IT'S A GOOD THING I BROUGHT THIS LITTLE NUMBER THEN.

NO WAY! IS THAT--

- -THE EVIL BLACK SUIT?!

YOU'D BETTER BELIEVE IT, BUCKO.

SHHLRP

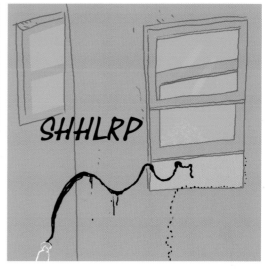

25

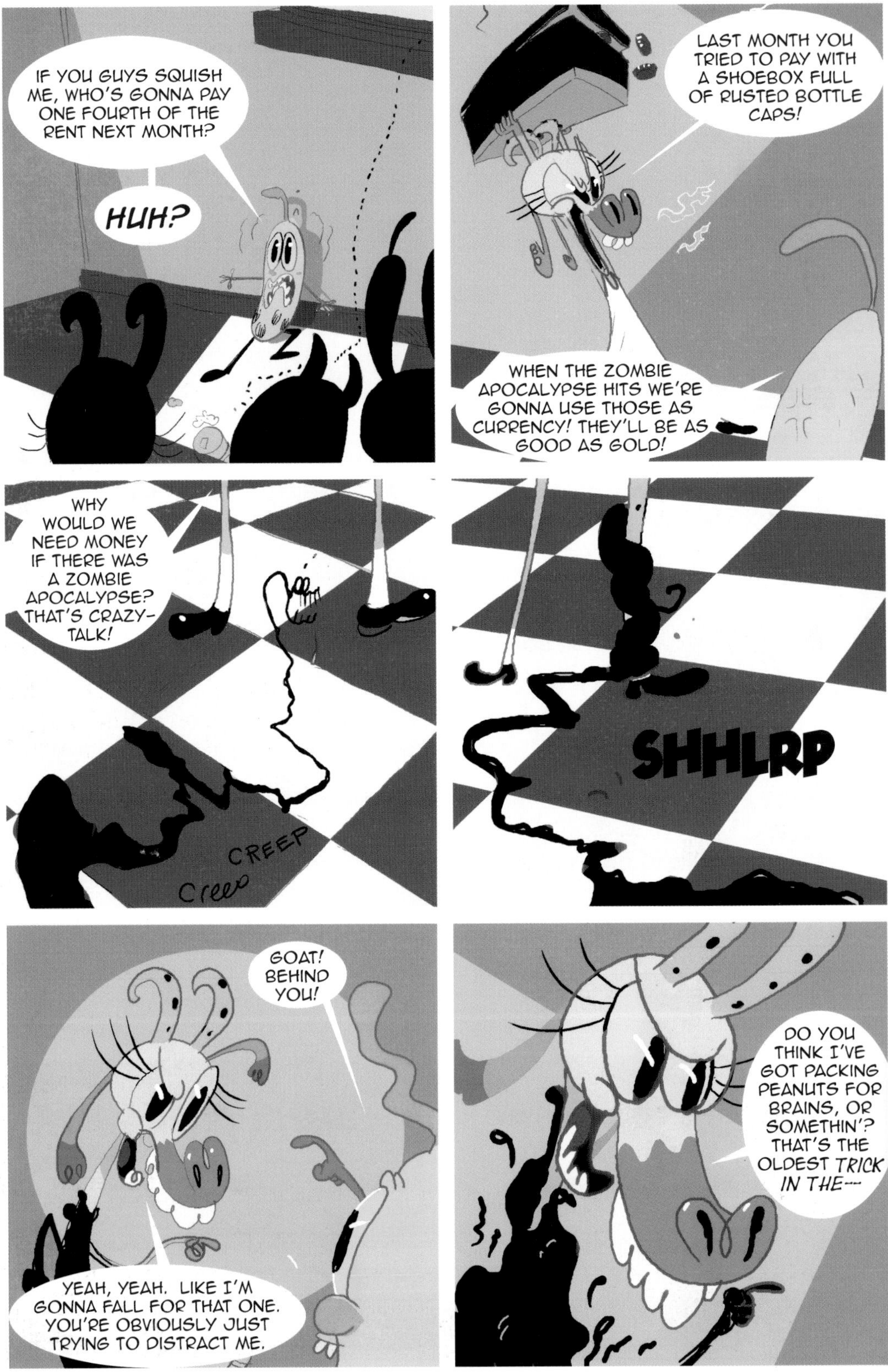
IF YOU GUYS SQUISH ME, WHO'S GONNA PAY ONE FOURTH OF THE RENT NEXT MONTH?
HUH?
LAST MONTH YOU TRIED TO PAY WITH A SHOEBOX FULL OF RUSTED BOTTLE CAPS!
WHEN THE ZOMBIE APOCALYPSE HITS WE'RE GONNA USE THOSE AS CURRENCY! THEY'LL BE AS GOOD AS GOLD!
WHY WOULD WE NEED MONEY IF THERE WAS A ZOMBIE APOCALYPSE? THAT'S CRAZY-TALK!
CREEP
Creep
SHHLRP
GOAT! BEHIND YOU!
YEAH, YEAH. LIKE I'M GONNA FALL FOR THAT ONE. YOU'RE OBVIOUSLY JUST TRYING TO DISTRACT ME.
DO YOU THINK I'VE GOT PACKING PEANUTS FOR BRAINS, OR SOMETHIN'? THAT'S THE OLDEST TRICK IN THE---

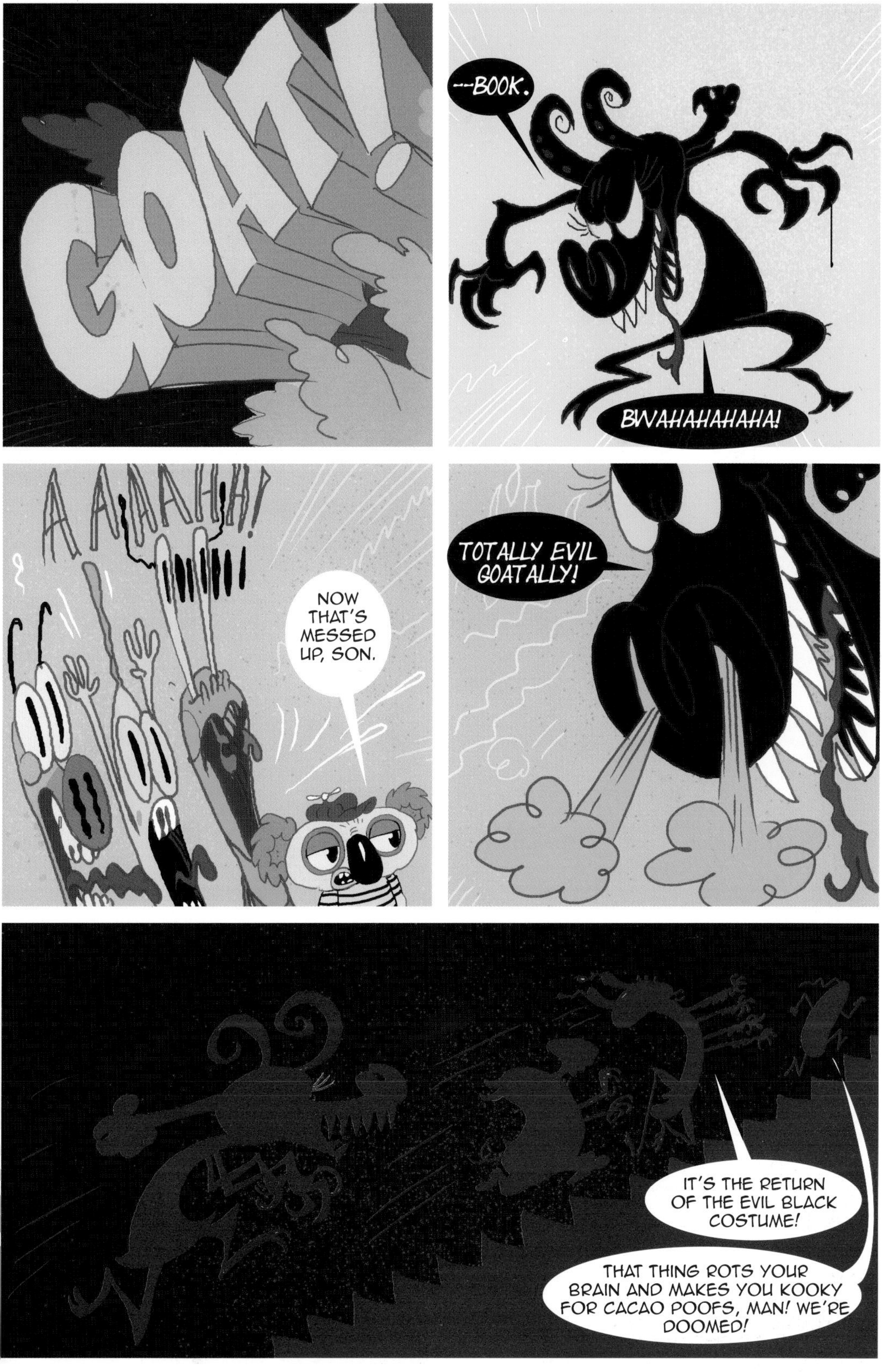
GOAT!
---BOOK.
BWAHAHAHAHA!
AAAAHH!
NOW THAT'S MESSED UP, SON.
TOTALLY EVIL GOATALLY!
IT'S THE RETURN OF THE EVIL BLACK COSTUME!
THAT THING ROTS YOUR BRAIN AND MAKES YOU KOOKY FOR CACAO POOFS, MAN! WE'RE DOOMED!

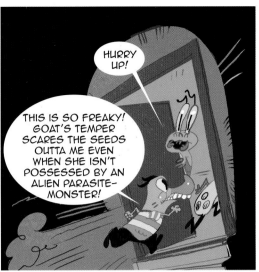

HURRY UP!

THIS IS SO FREAKY! GOAT'S TEMPER SCARES THE SEEDS OUTTA ME EVEN WHEN SHE ISN'T POSSESSED BY AN ALIEN PARASITE-MONSTER!

PIG, DON'T EVEN GET ME STARTED ABOUT HOW YOU ALWAYS LEAVE THE SEAT UP IN THE BATHROOM!

WHEW.

BUT THAT'S IMPOSSIBLE! HOW COULD I LEAVE THE SEAT UP? I PEE SITTING DOWN!

THAT'S WHAT I'M SAYIN'! I DIDN'T EVEN HAVE PEANUT BUTTER FOR DINNER LAST NIGHT.

SOMETHING REAL SCREWY IS GOIN' ON...

SPLORP

YOU SAYIN' SOMEBODY-- OR SOMETHING-- SET US UP?

?

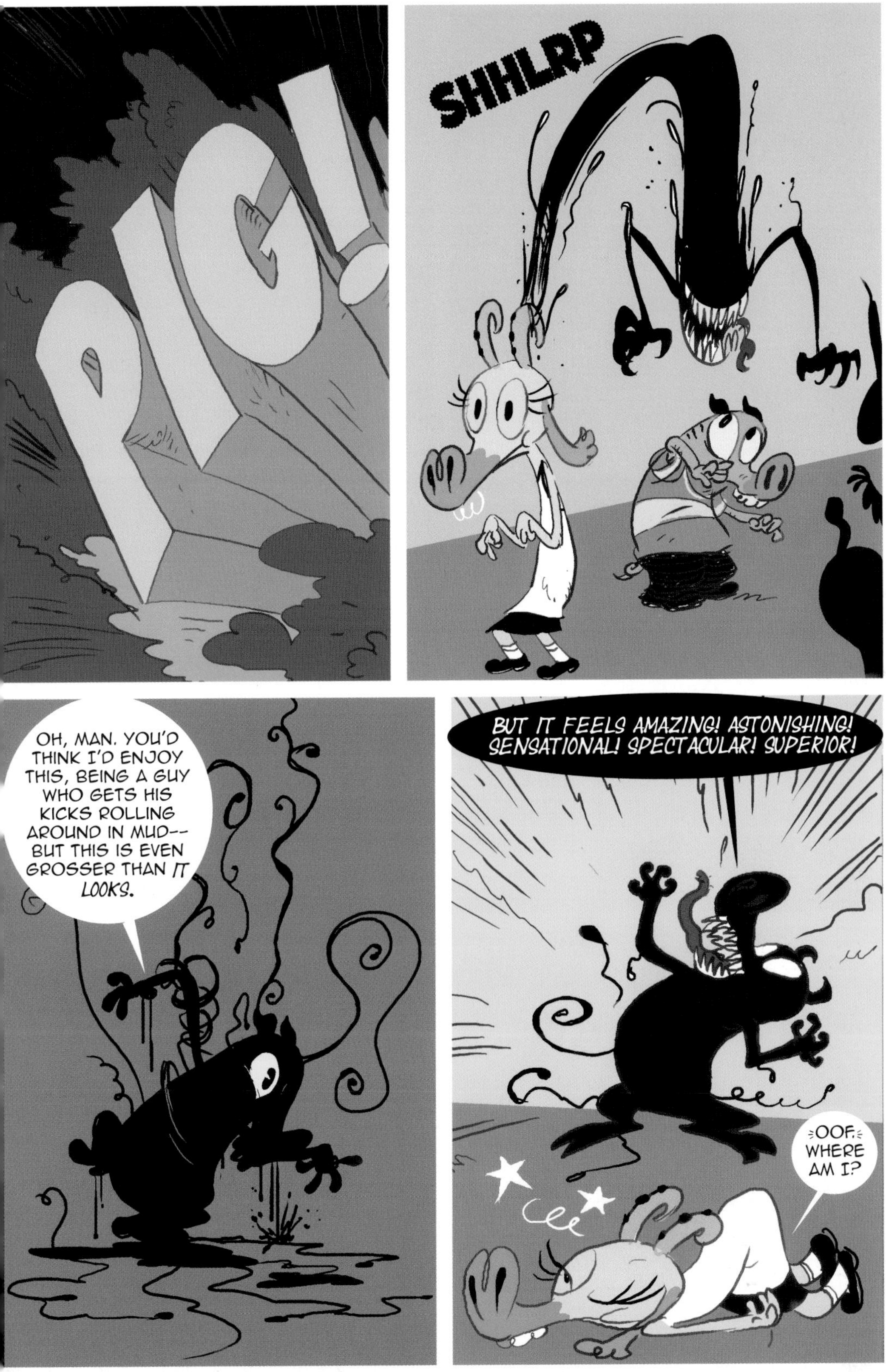
PIG!
SHHLRP
OH, MAN. YOU'D THINK I'D ENJOY THIS, BEING A GUY WHO GETS HIS KICKS ROLLING AROUND IN MUD-- BUT THIS IS EVEN GROSSER THAN IT LOOKS.
BUT IT FEELS AMAZING! ASTONISHING! SENSATIONAL! SPECTACULAR! SUPERIOR!
OOF. WHERE AM I?

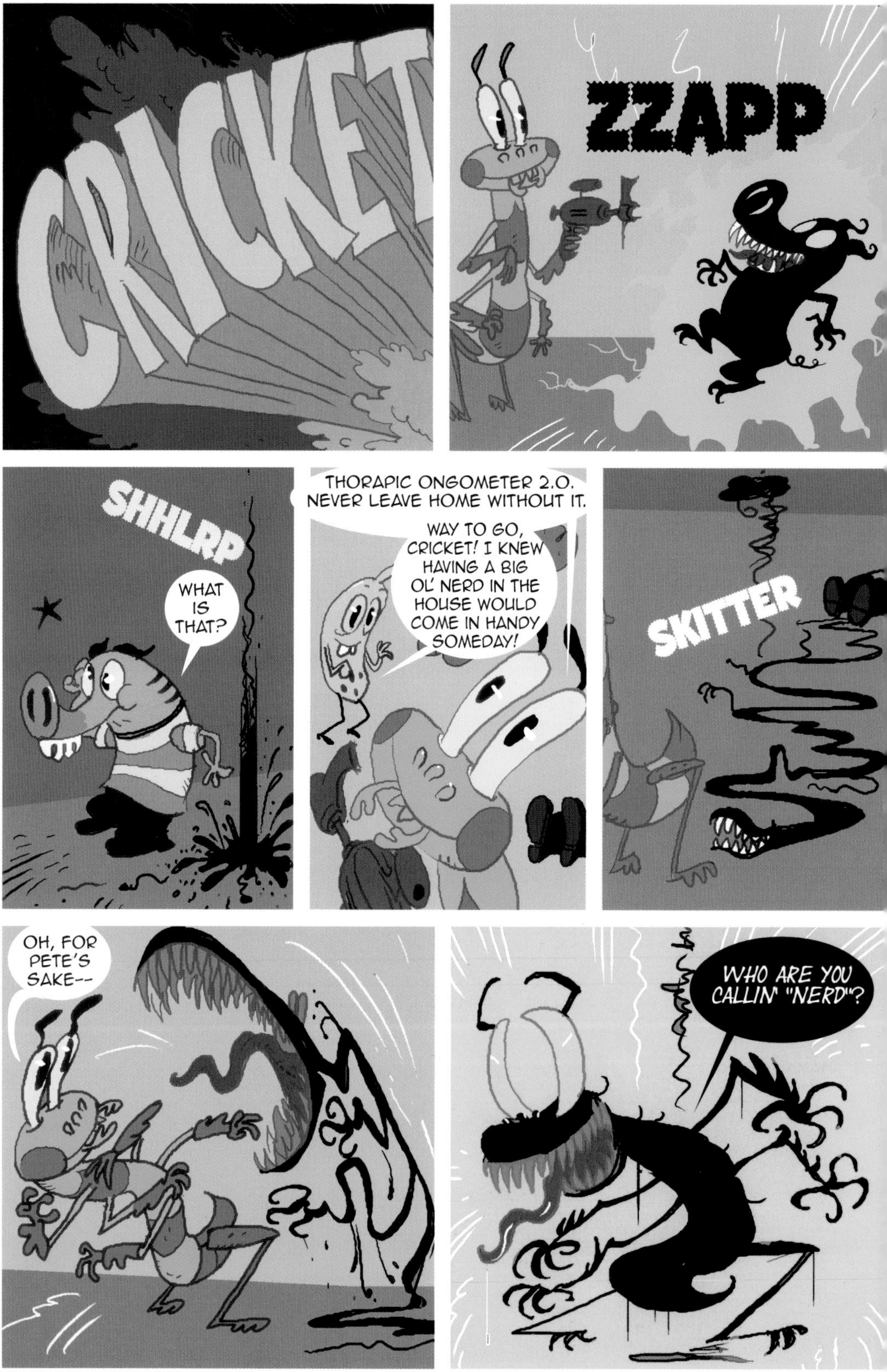
CRICKET
ZZAPP
SHHLRP
WHAT IS THAT?
THORAPIC ONGOMETER 2.0. NEVER LEAVE HOME WITHOUT IT.
WAY TO GO, CRICKET! I KNEW HAVING A BIG OL' NERD IN THE HOUSE WOULD COME IN HANDY SOMEDAY!
SKITTER
OH, FOR PETE'S SAKE--
WHO ARE YOU CALLIN' "NERD"?

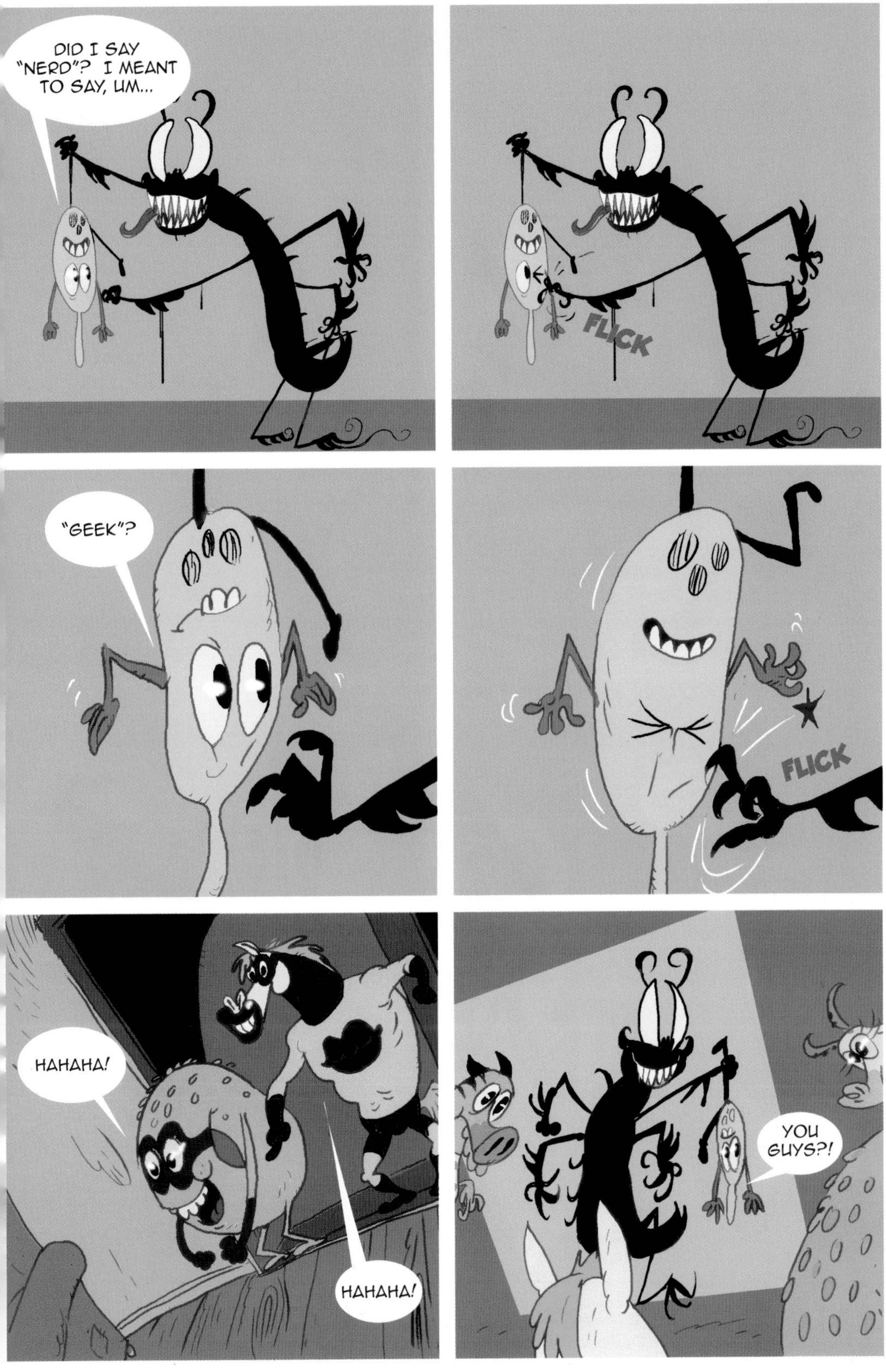
DID I SAY "NERD"? I MEANT TO SAY, UM...
FLICK
"GEEK"?
FLICK
HAHAHA!
HAHAHA!
YOU GUYS?!

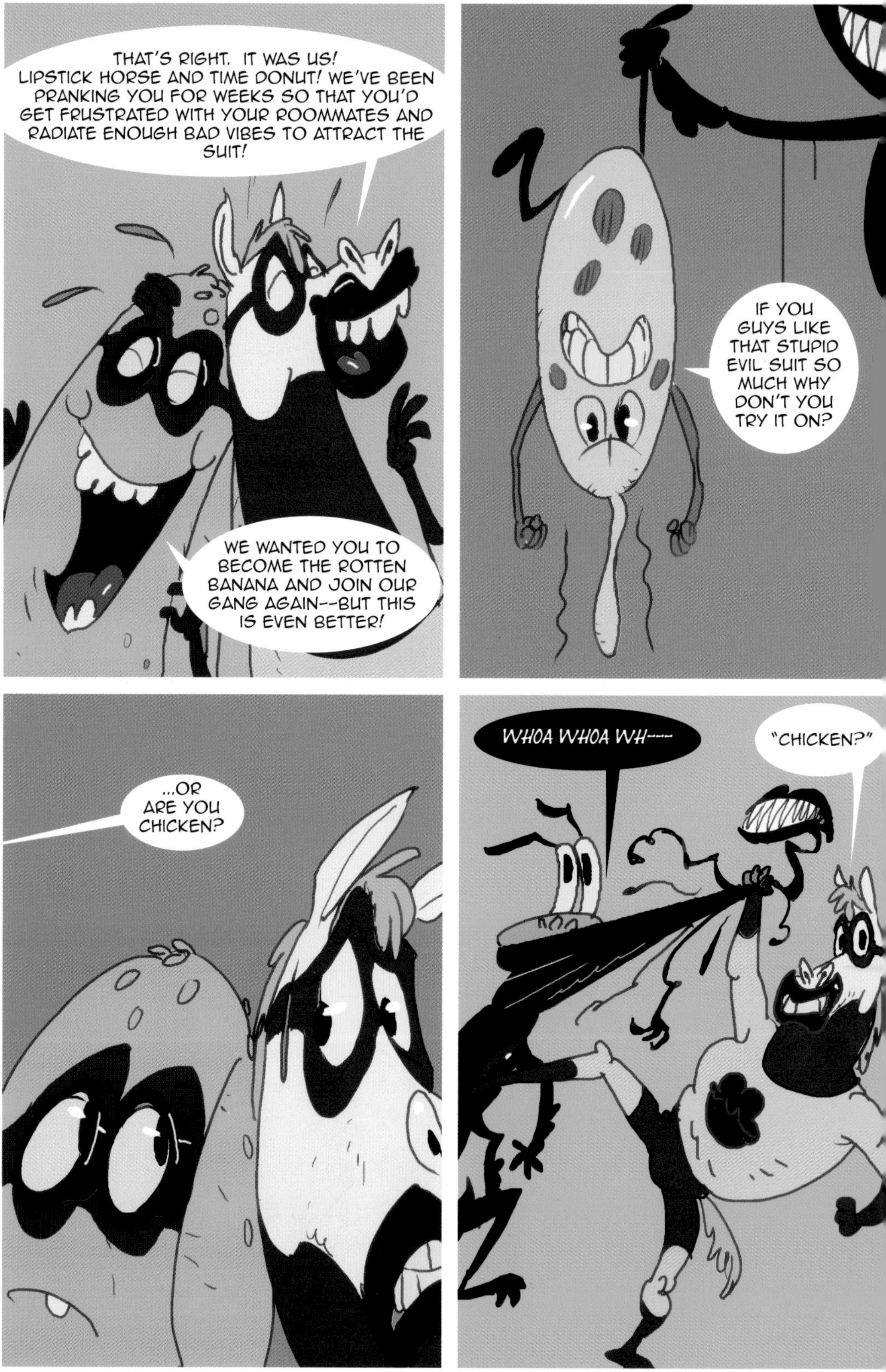
THAT'S RIGHT. IT WAS US! LIPSTICK HORSE AND TIME DONUT! WE'VE BEEN PRANKING YOU FOR WEEKS SO THAT YOU'D GET FRUSTRATED WITH YOUR ROOMMATES AND RADIATE ENOUGH BAD VIBES TO ATTRACT THE SUIT!
WE WANTED YOU TO BECOME THE ROTTEN BANANA AND JOIN OUR GANG AGAIN--BUT THIS IS EVEN BETTER!
IF YOU GUYS LIKE THAT STUPID EVIL SUIT SO MUCH WHY DON'T YOU TRY IT ON?
...OR ARE YOU CHICKEN?
WHOA WHOA WH----
"CHICKEN?"

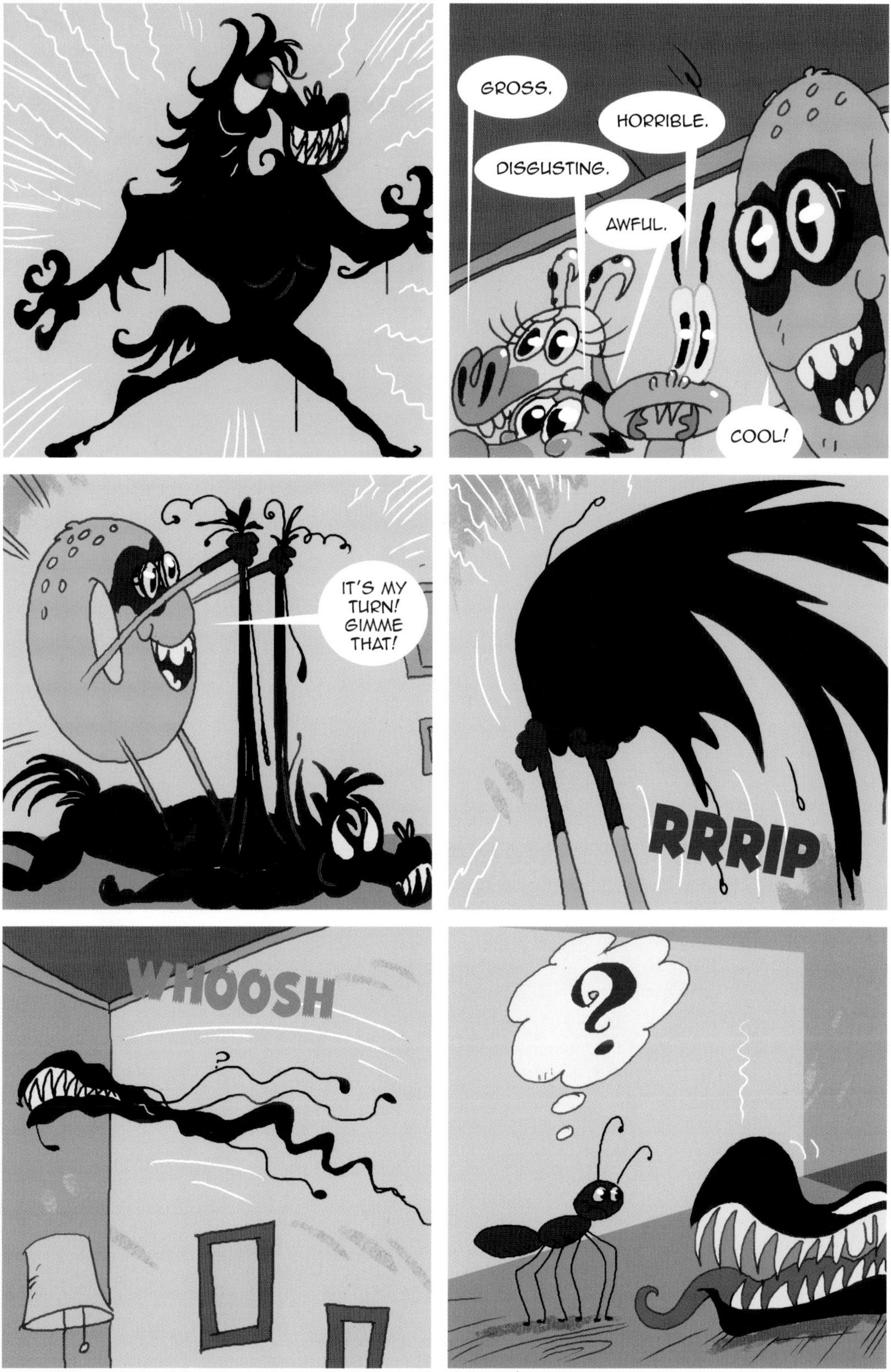
GROSS.
HORRIBLE.
DISGUSTING.
AWFUL.
COOL!
IT'S MY TURN! GIMME THAT!
RRRIP
WHOOSH
?
?

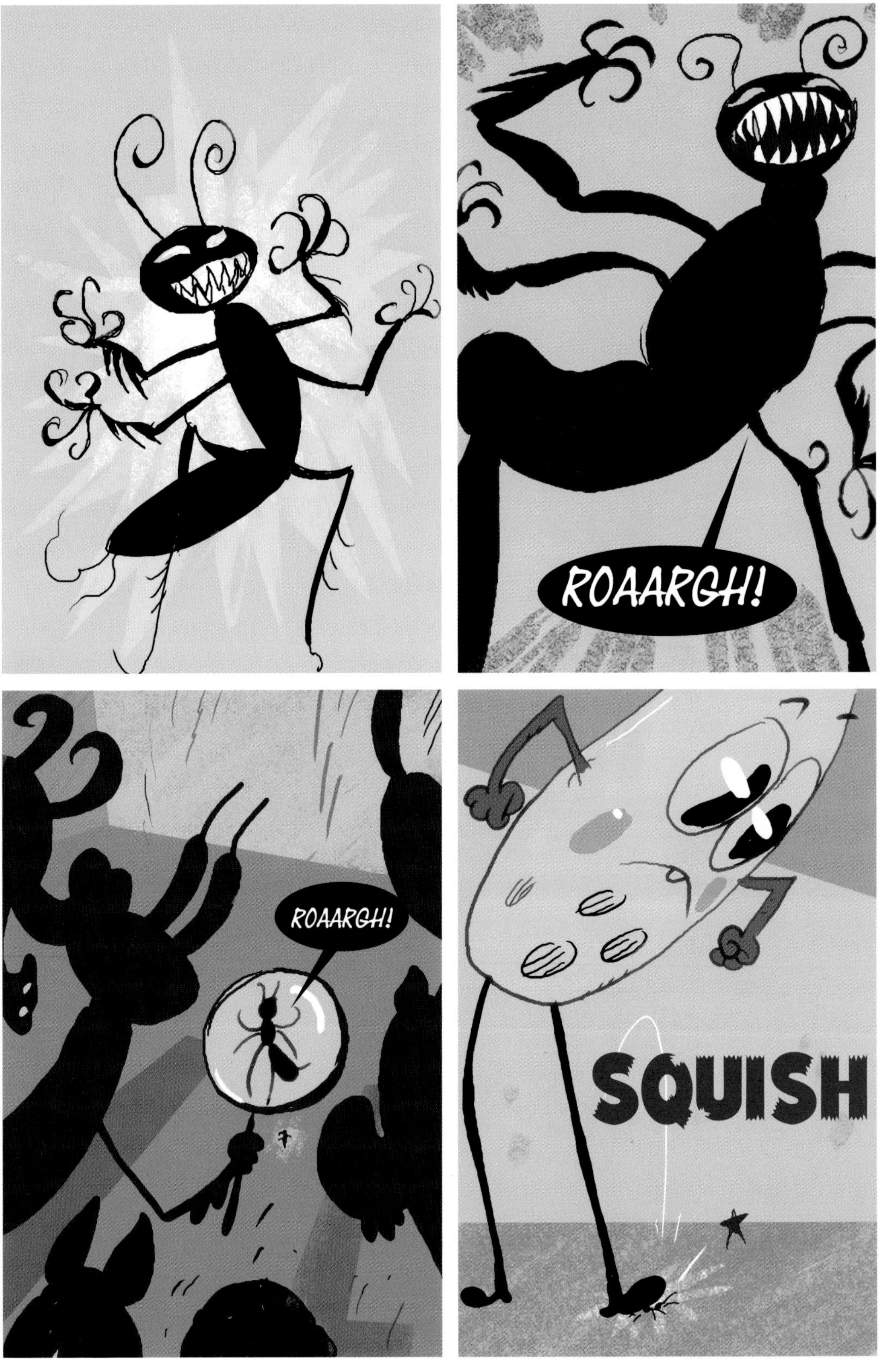
ROAARGH!
ROAARGH!
SQUISH

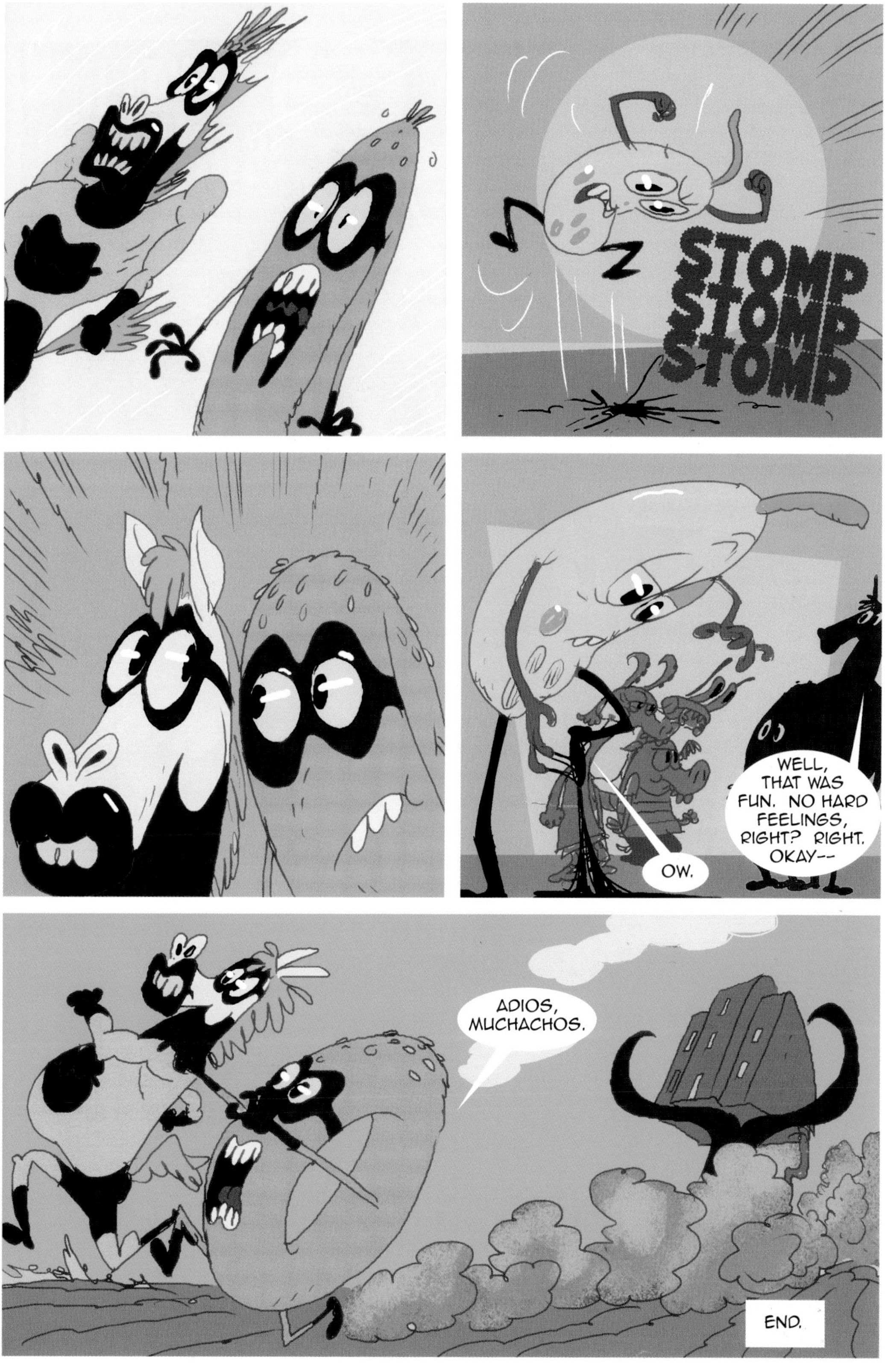
STOMP STOMP STOMP
OW.
WELL, THAT WAS FUN. NO HARD FEELINGS, RIGHT? RIGHT. OKAY--
ADIOS, MUCHACHOS.
END.

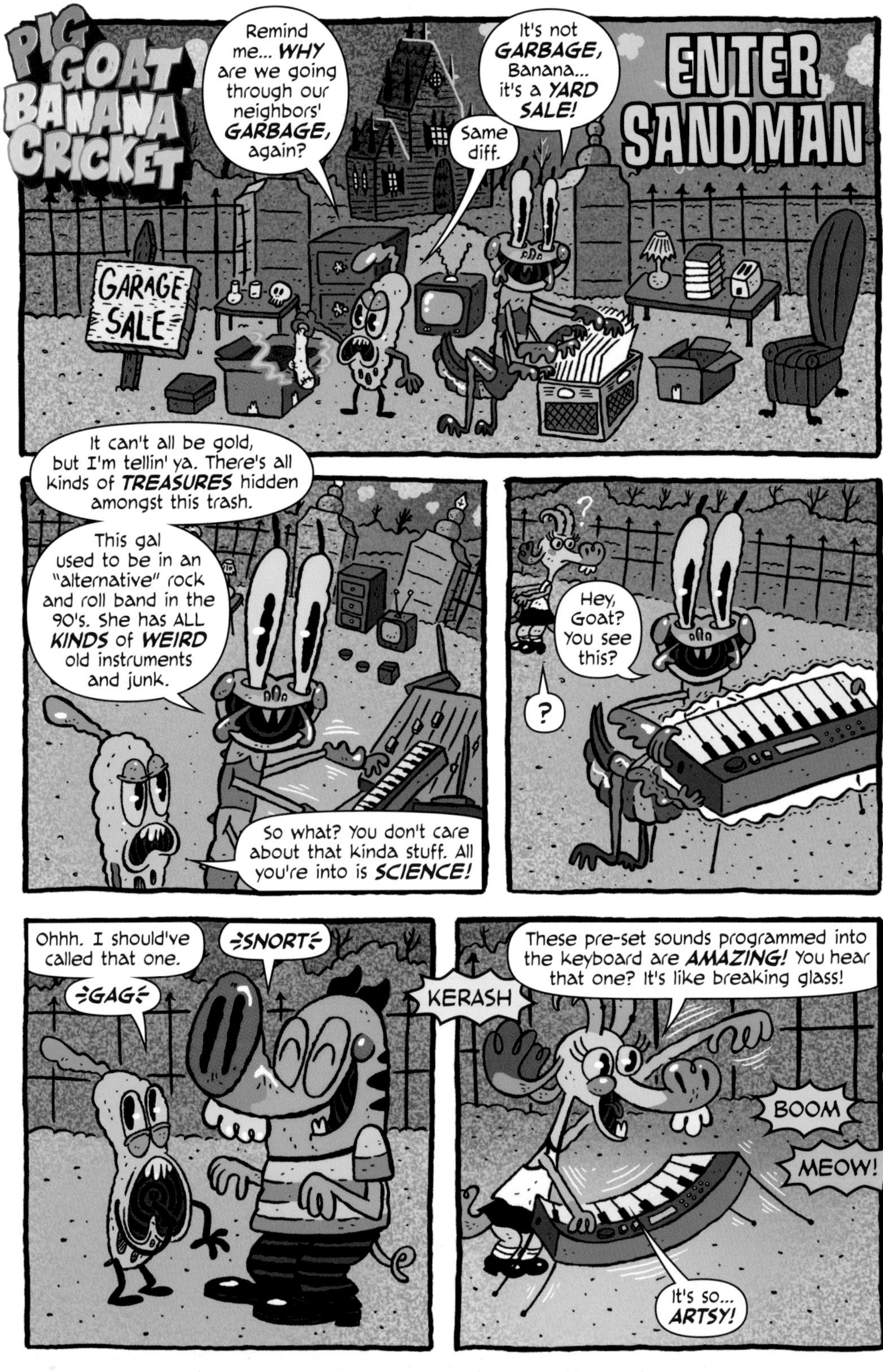

PIG GOAT BANANA CRICKET
ENTER SANDMAN
Remind me... WHY are we going through our neighbors' GARBAGE, again?
It's not GARBAGE, Banana... it's a YARD SALE!
Same diff.
GARAGE SALE
It can't all be gold, but I'm tellin' ya. There's all kinds of TREASURES hidden amongst this trash.
This gal used to be in an "alternative" rock and roll band in the 90's. She has ALL KINDS of WEIRD old instruments and junk.
So what? You don't care about that kinda stuff. All you're into is SCIENCE!
?
Hey, Goat? You see this?
?
Ohhh. I should've called that one.
GAG
SNORT
These pre-set sounds programmed into the keyboard are AMAZING! You hear that one? It's like breaking glass!
KERASH
BOOM
MEOW!
It's so... ARTSY!

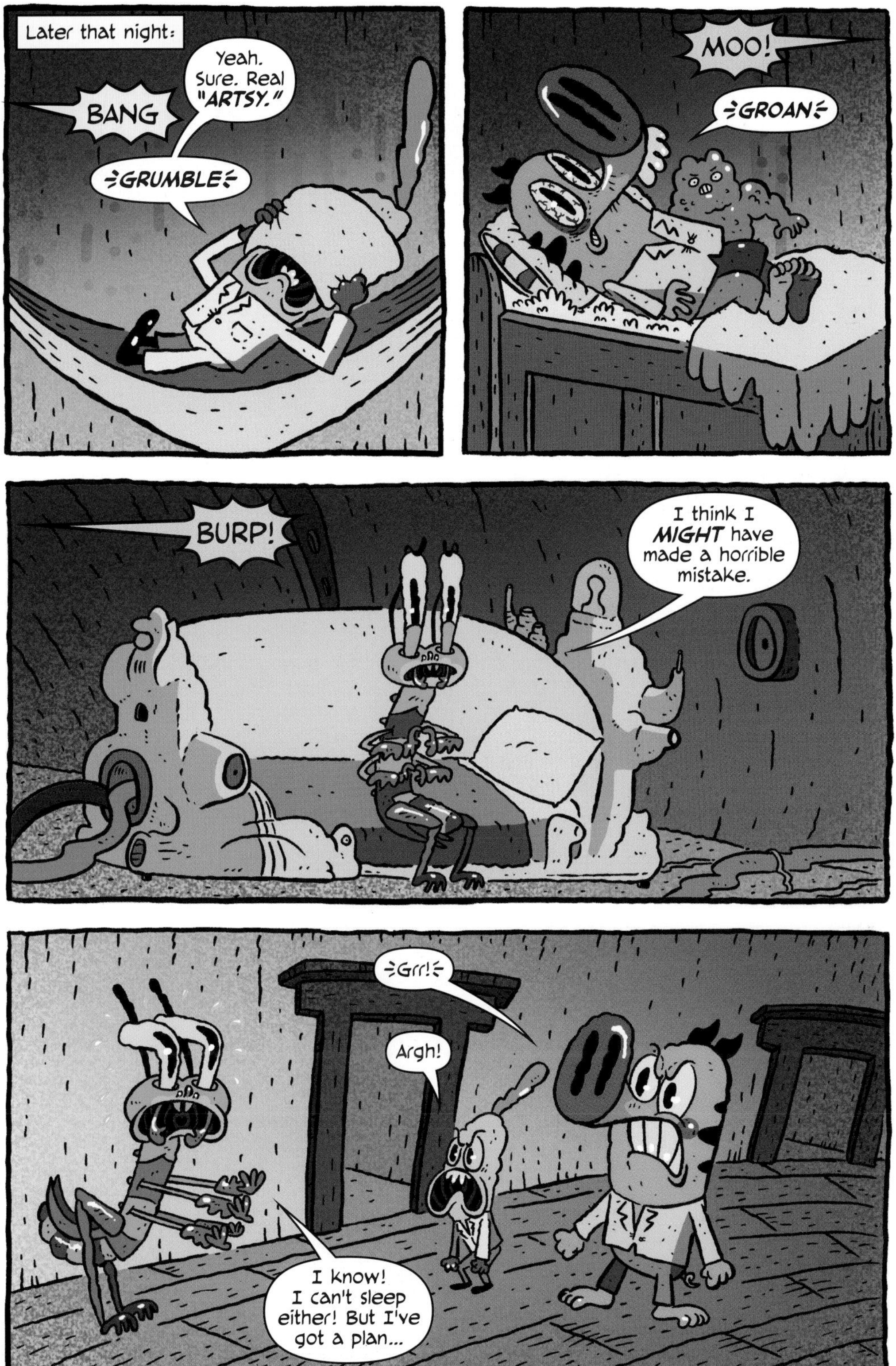
Later that night:
BANG
Yeah. Sure. Real "ARTSY."
GRUMBLE
MOO!
GROAN
BURP!
I think I MIGHT have made a horrible mistake.
Grr!
Argh!
I know! I can't sleep either! But I've got a plan...

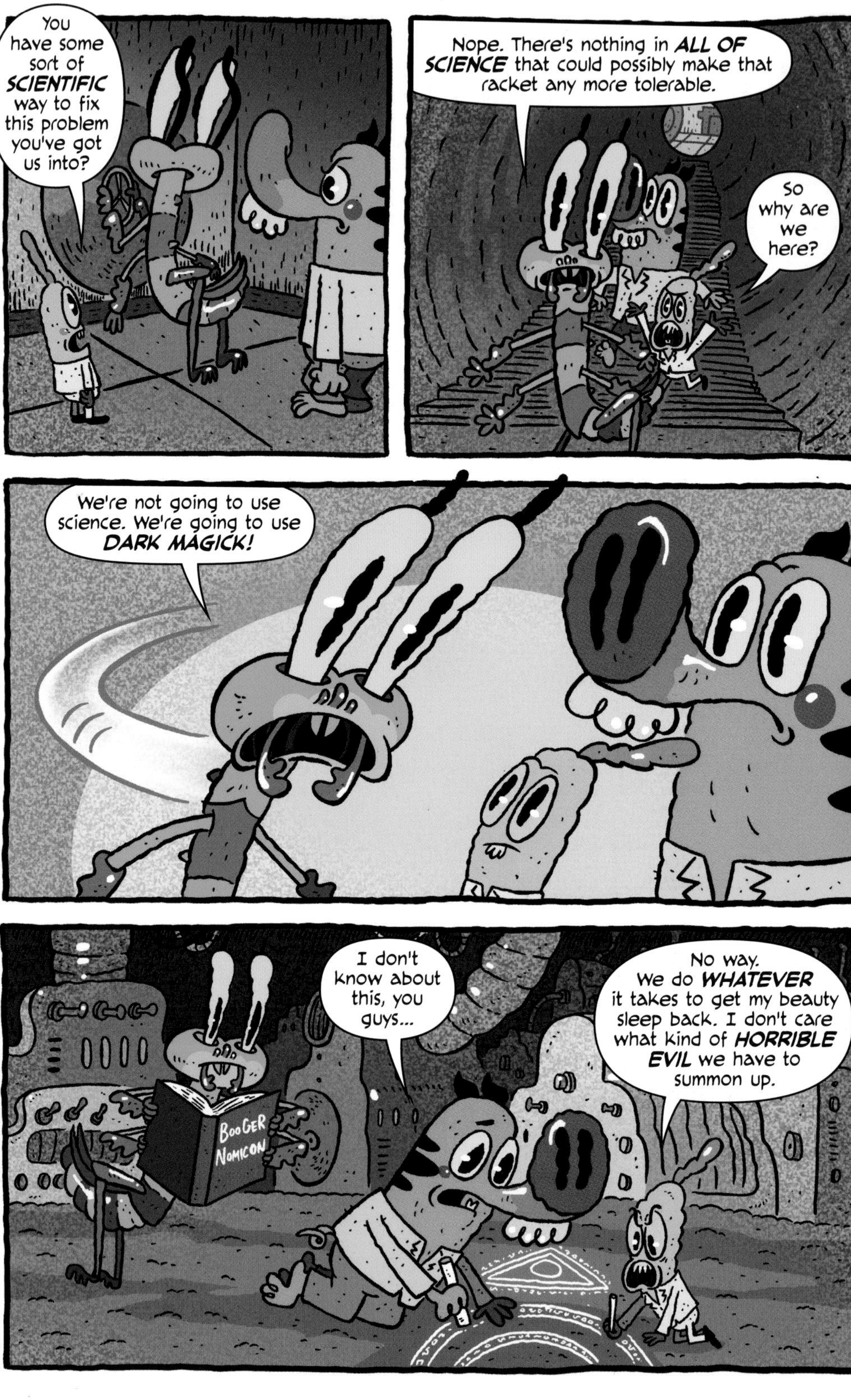
You have some sort of SCIENTIFIC way to fix this problem you've got us into?
Nope. There's nothing in ALL OF SCIENCE that could possibly make that racket any more tolerable.
So why are we here?
We're not going to use science. We're going to use DARK MAGICK!
I don't know about this, you guys...
No way. We do WHATEVER it takes to get my beauty sleep back. I don't care what kind of HORRIBLE EVIL we have to summon up.
BooGER NomICON

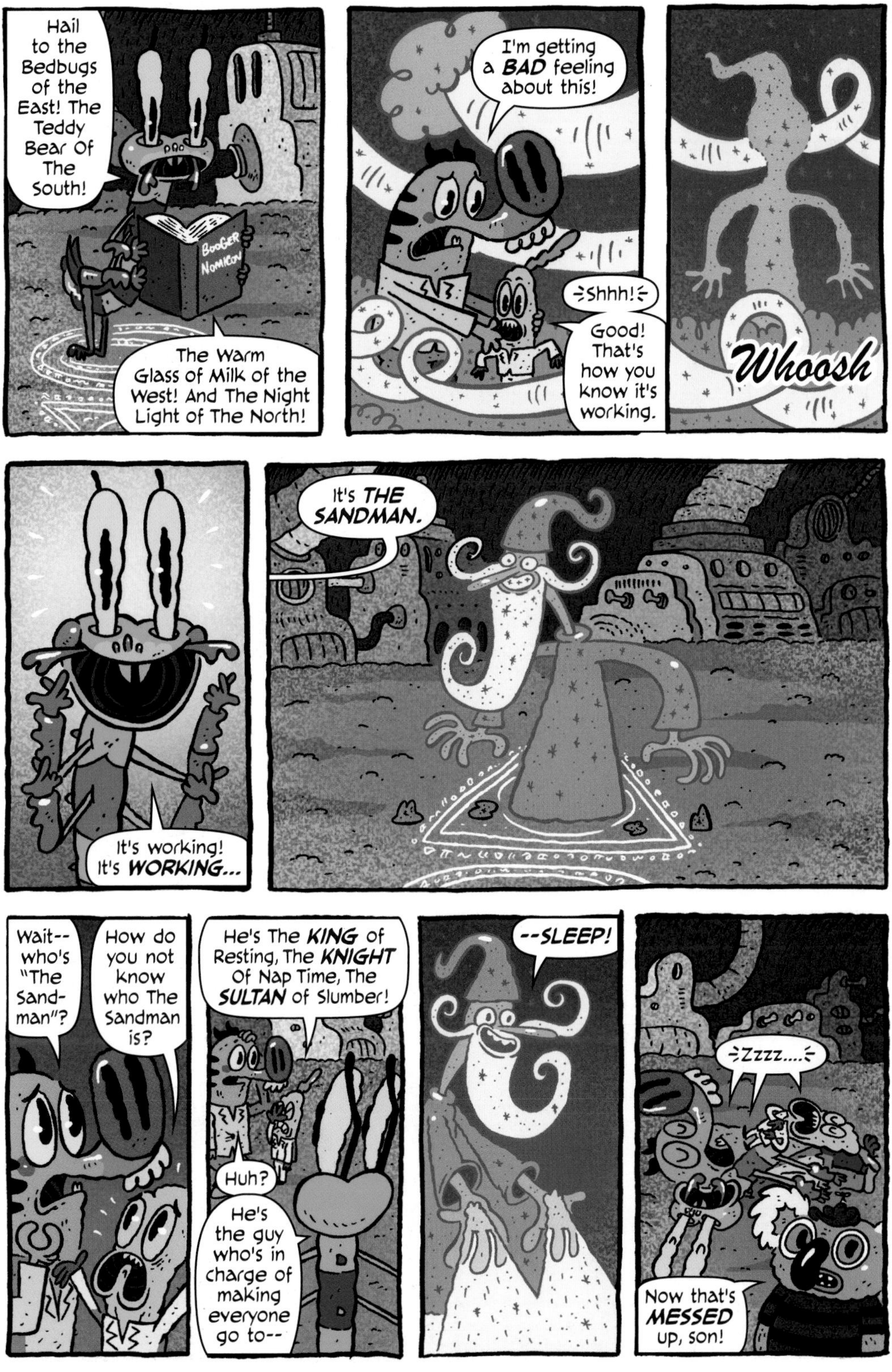
Hail to the Bedbugs of the East! The Teddy Bear Of The South!
BOOGER NOMICON
The Warm Glass of Milk of the West! And The Night Light of The North!
I'm getting a BAD feeling about this!
Shhh!
Good! That's how you know it's working.
Whoosh
It's working! It's WORKING...
It's THE SANDMAN.
Wait-- who's "The Sand-man"?
How do you not know who The Sandman is?
He's The KING of Resting, The KNIGHT Of Nap Time, The SULTAN of Slumber!
Huh?
He's the guy who's in charge of making everyone go to--
--SLEEP!
Zzzz....
Now that's MESSED up, son!

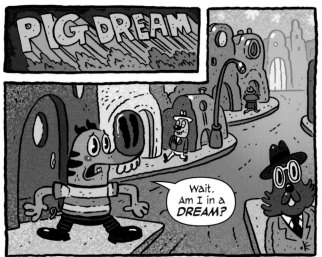

PIG DREAM

Wait. Am I in a **DREAM?**

WHEE-OO WHEE-OO

Dream crime!

WHAM

DESTROYER DILL! You're my **FAVORITE** hero!

I'm glad to hear it, chum!

Really?

Really! I'm gonna need some help catching these bad guys. You game?

Am I?

This is a **DREAM** come true!

Heh.

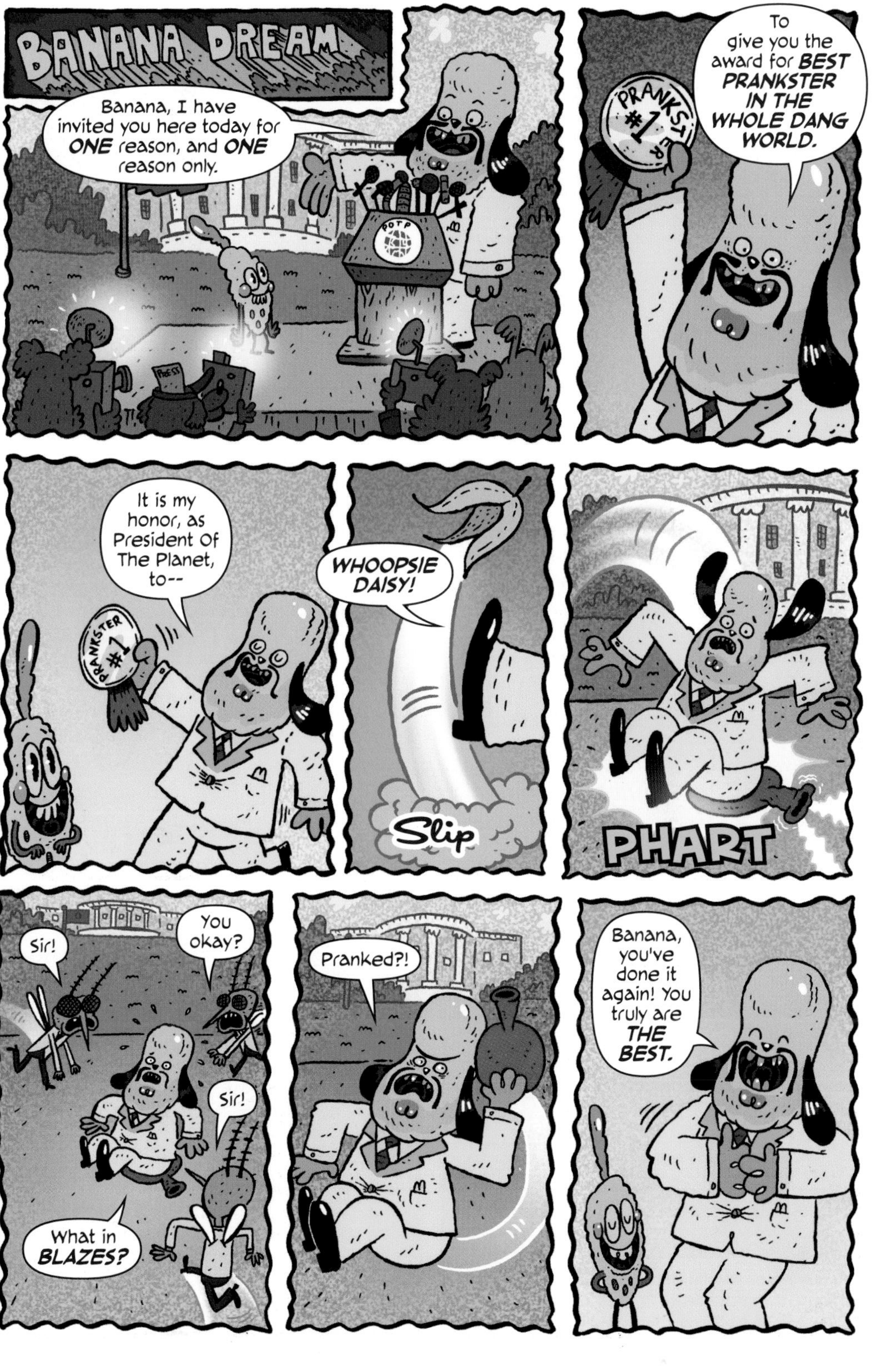
BANANA DREAM
Banana, I have invited you here today for ONE reason, and ONE reason only.
To give you the award for BEST PRANKSTER IN THE WHOLE DANG WORLD.
PRANKSTER #1
It is my honor, as President Of The Planet, to--
PRANKSTER #1
WHOOPSIE DAISY!
Slip
PHART
Sir!
You okay?
Sir!
What in BLAZES?
Pranked?!
Banana, you've done it again! You truly are THE BEST.

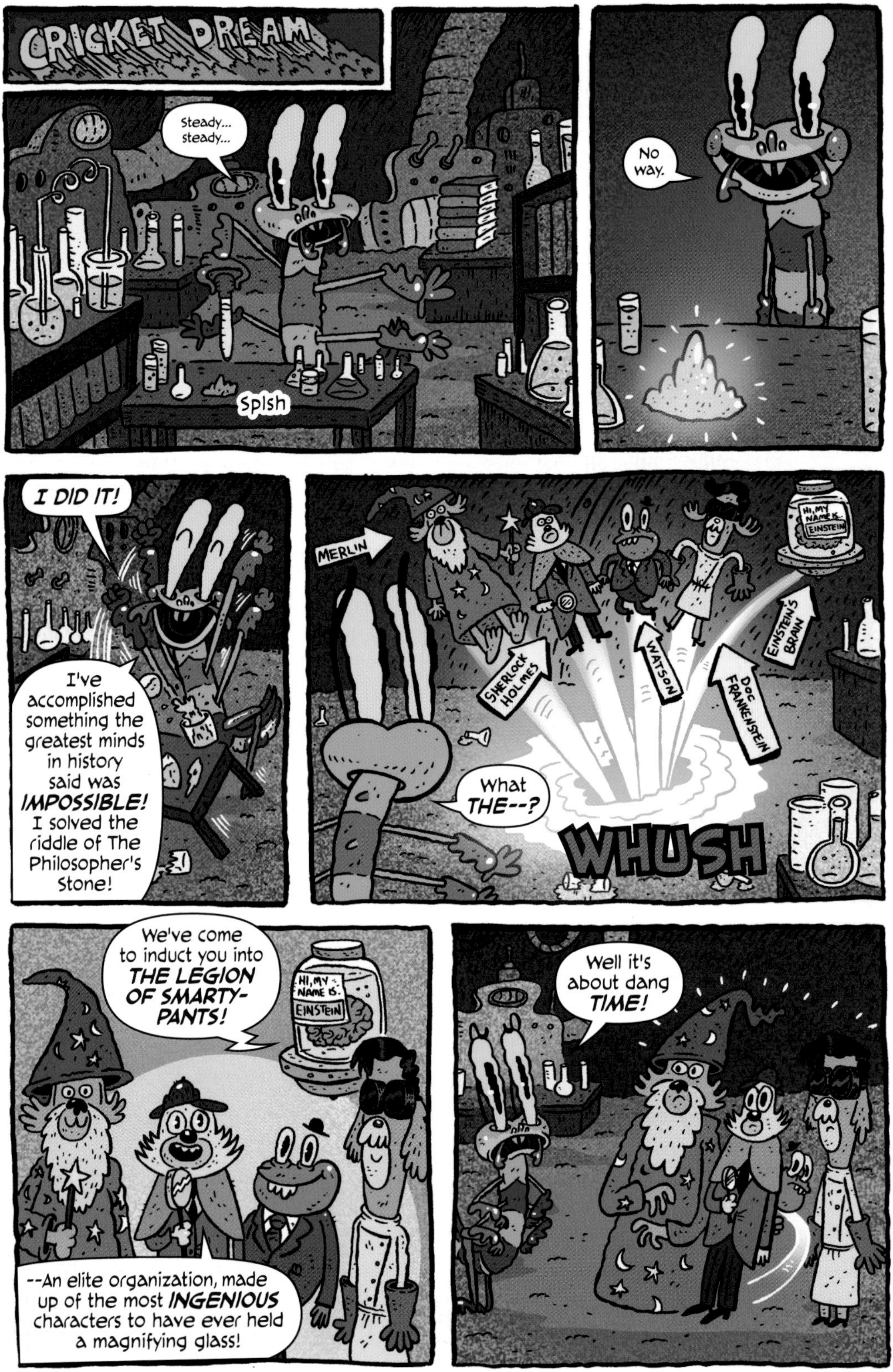

CRICKET DREAM
Steady... steady...
Splsh
No way.
I DID IT!
I've accomplished something the greatest minds in history said was IMPOSSIBLE! I solved the riddle of The Philosopher's Stone!
MERLIN
SHERLOCK HOLMES
WATSON
DOC FRANKENSTEIN
EINSTEIN'S BRAIN
HI, MY NAME IS: EINSTEIN
What THE--?
WHUSH
We've come to induct you into THE LEGION OF SMARTY-PANTS!
HI, MY NAME IS: EINSTEIN
--An elite organization, made up of the most INGENIOUS characters to have ever held a magnifying glass!
Well it's about dang TIME!

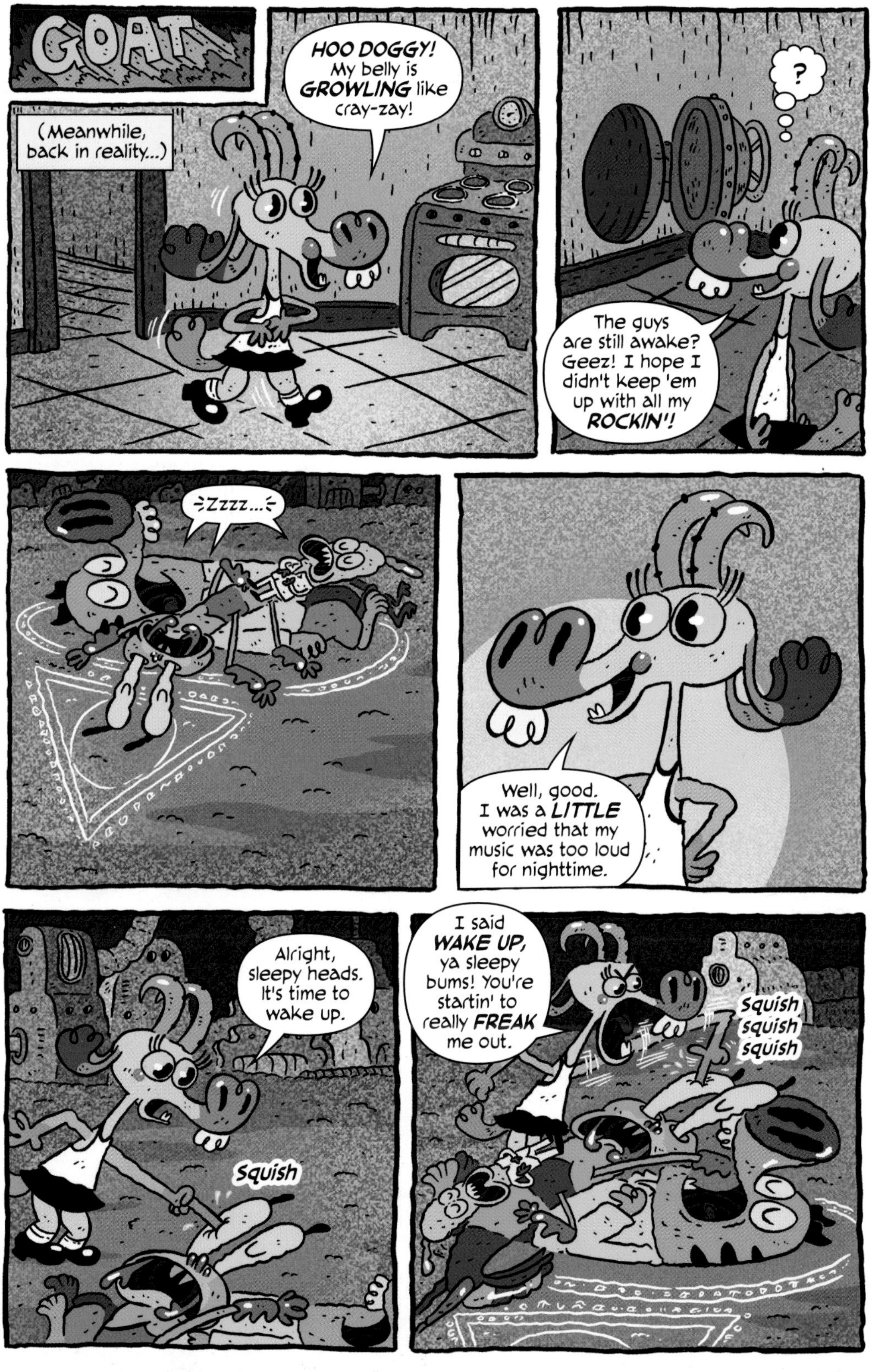
GOAT
(Meanwhile, back in reality...)
HOO DOGGY! My belly is GROWLING like cray-zay!
?
The guys are still awake? Geez! I hope I didn't keep 'em up with all my ROCKIN'!
Zzzz...
Well, good. I was a LITTLE worried that my music was too loud for nighttime.
Alright, sleepy heads. It's time to wake up.
Squish
I said WAKE UP, ya sleepy bums! You're startin' to really FREAK me out.
Squish squish squish

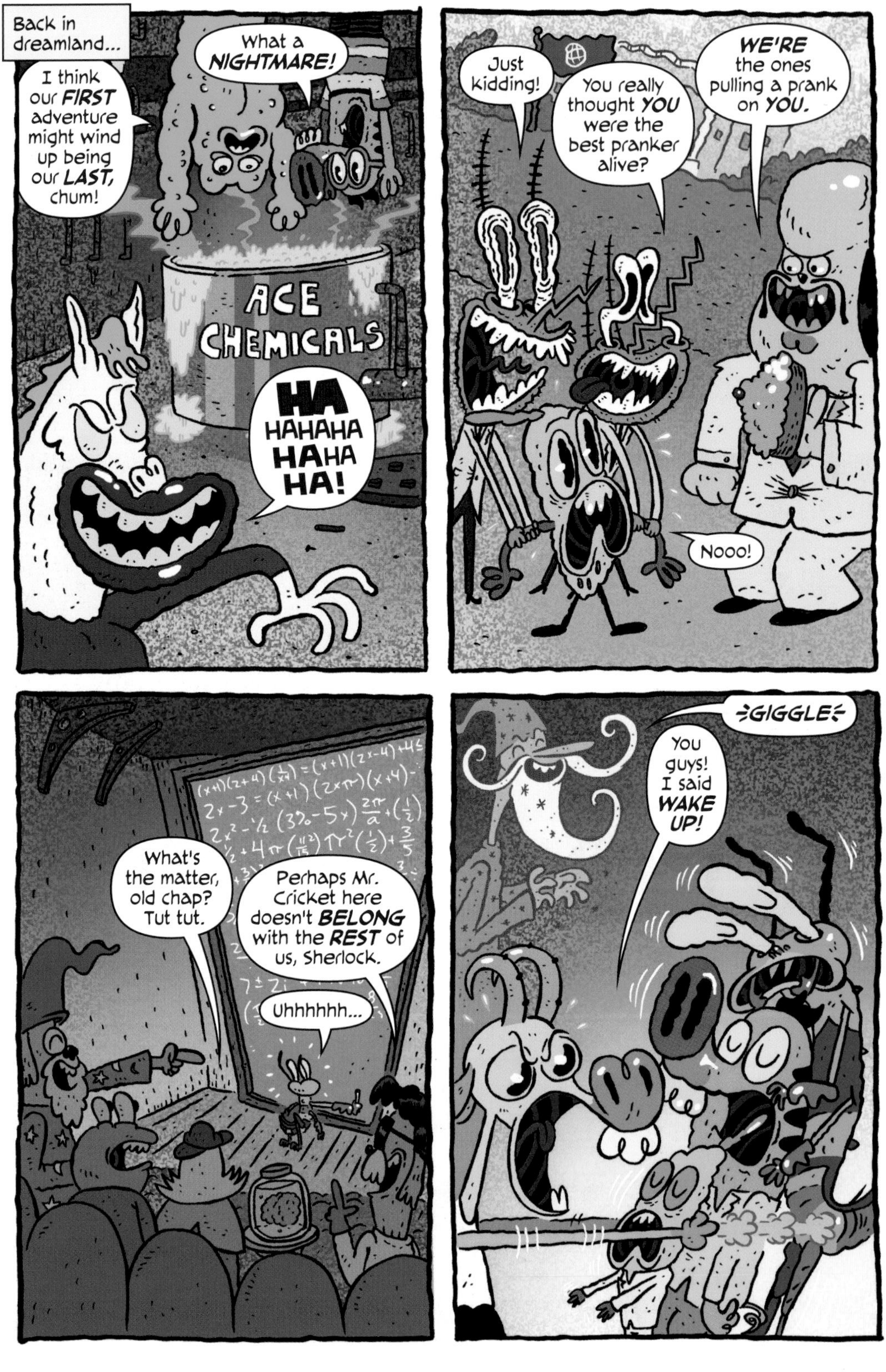
Back in dreamland...
I think our FIRST adventure might wind up being our LAST, chum!
What a NIGHTMARE!
ACE CHEMICALS
HA HAHAHA HAHAHA HA!
Just kidding!
You really thought YOU were the best pranker alive?
WE'RE the ones pulling a prank on YOU.
Nooo!
What's the matter, old chap? Tut tut.
Perhaps Mr. Cricket here doesn't BELONG with the REST of us, Sherlock.
Uhhhhhh...
GIGGLE
You guys! I said WAKE UP!

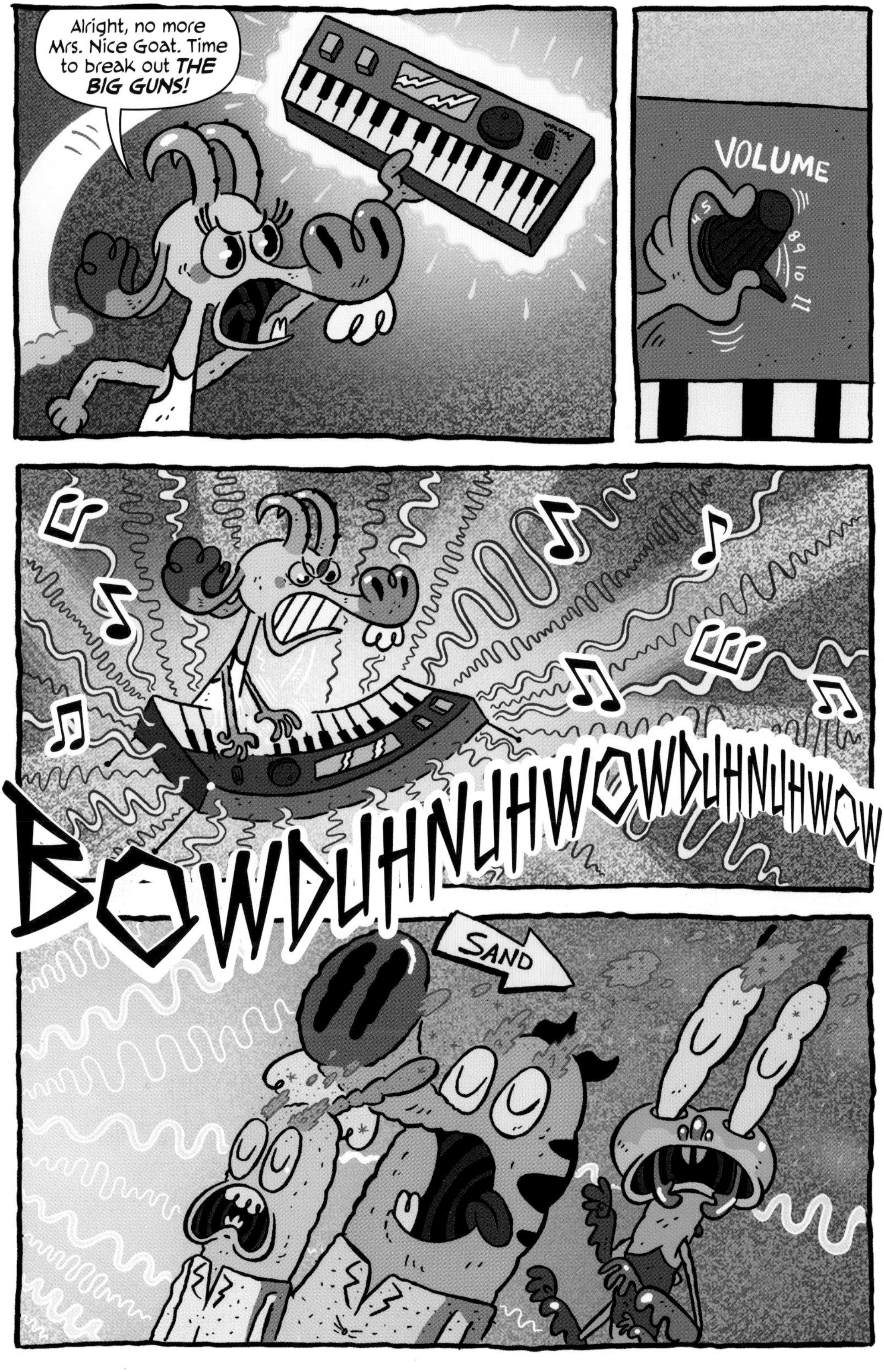
Alright, no more Mrs. Nice Goat. Time to break out THE BIG GUNS!
VOLUME
VOLUME
4 5
8 9 10 11
BOWDUHNUHWOWDUHNUHWOW
SAND

Oh

My

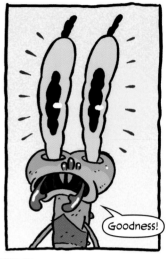

Goodness!

NO!

What's the matter with you? You're messin' with all my *HARD WORK!*

What'd you do to my friends?

NOTHIN' compared to what I'm gonna do to *YOU!*

Is that right?

Yeah!

Y'sure?

Sure as I've ever been!

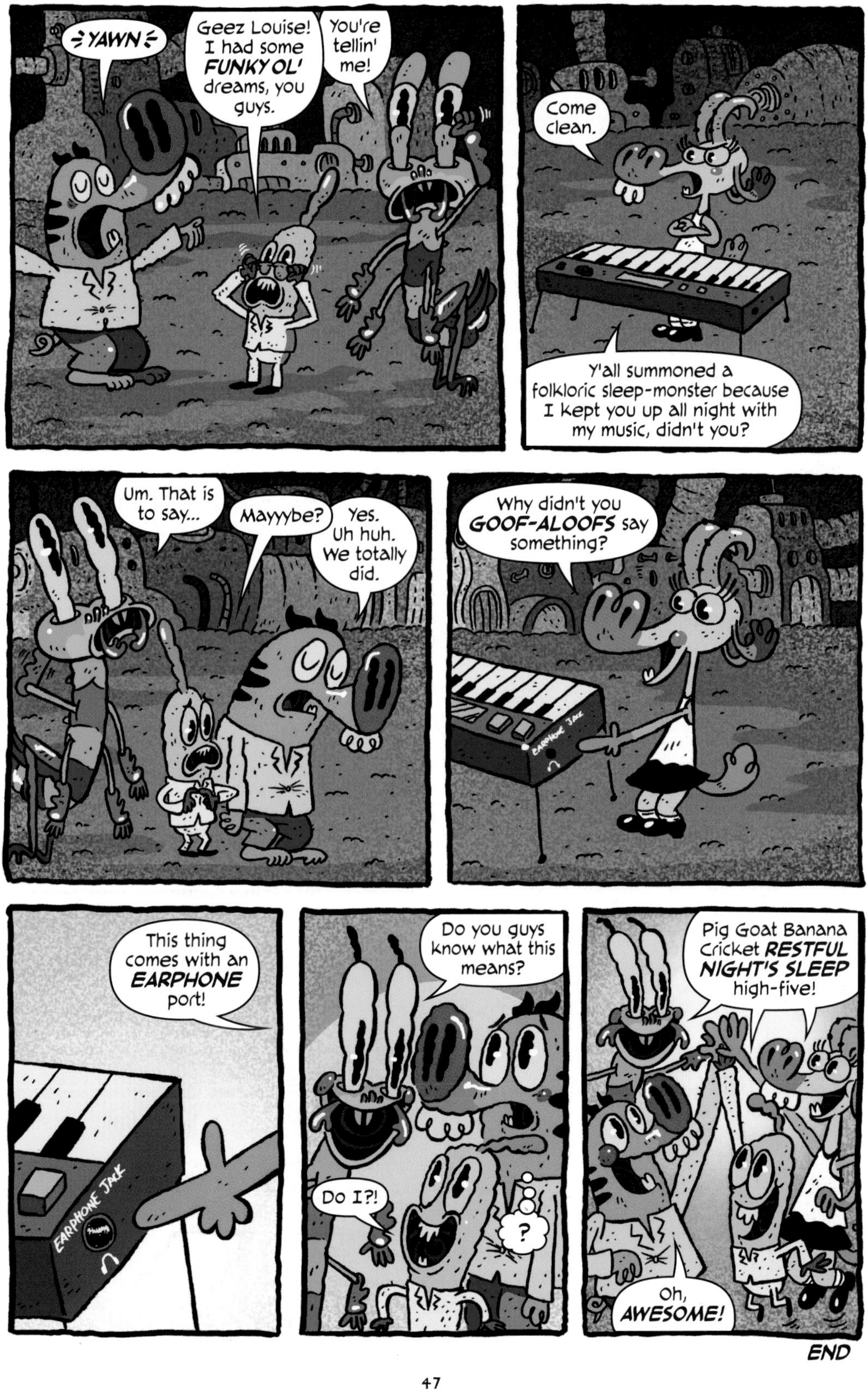

YAWN
Geez Louise! I had some FUNKY OL' dreams, you guys.
You're tellin' me!
Come clean.
Y'all summoned a folkloric sleep-monster because I kept you up all night with my music, didn't you?
Um. That is to say...
Mayyybe?
Yes. Uh huh. We totally did.
Why didn't you GOOF-ALOOFS say something?
EARPHONE JACK
This thing comes with an EARPHONE port!
EARPHONE JACK
Do you guys know what this means?
Do I?!
?
Pig Goat Banana Cricket RESTFUL NIGHT'S SLEEP high-five!
Oh, AWESOME!
END

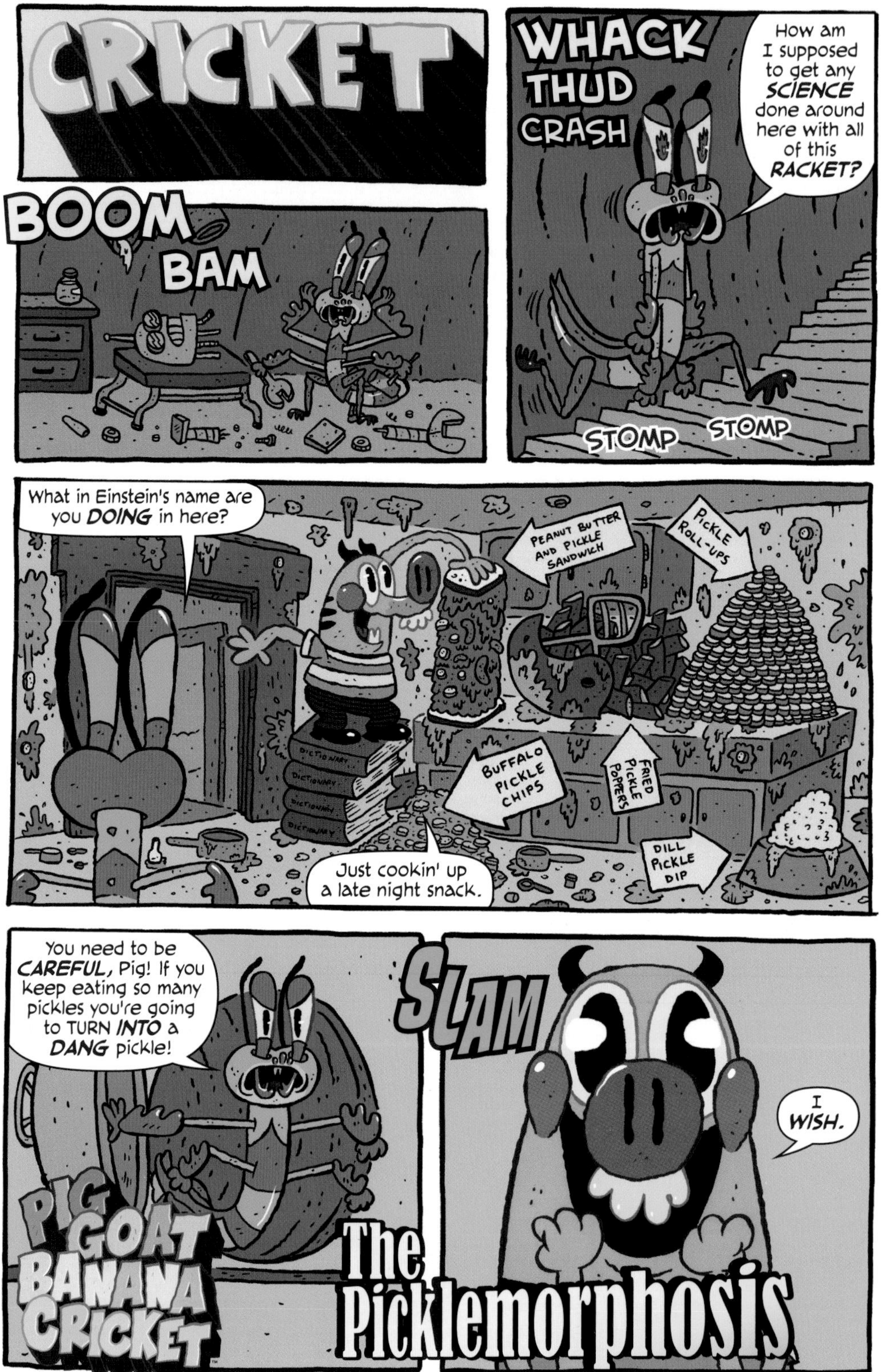
CRICKET
BOOM
BAM
WHACK
THUD
CRASH
How am I supposed to get any SCIENCE done around here with all of this RACKET?
STOMP
STOMP
What in Einstein's name are you DOING in here?
PEANUT BUTTER AND PICKLE SANDWICH
PICKLE ROLL-UPS
DICTIONARY
DICTIONARY
DICTIONARY
DICTIONARY
BUFFALO PICKLE CHIPS
FRIED PICKLE POPPERS
DILL PICKLE DIP
Just cookin' up a late night snack.
You need to be CAREFUL, Pig! If you keep eating so many pickles you're going to TURN INTO a DANG pickle!
SLAM
I WISH.
PIG GOAT BANANA CRICKET
The Picklemorphosis

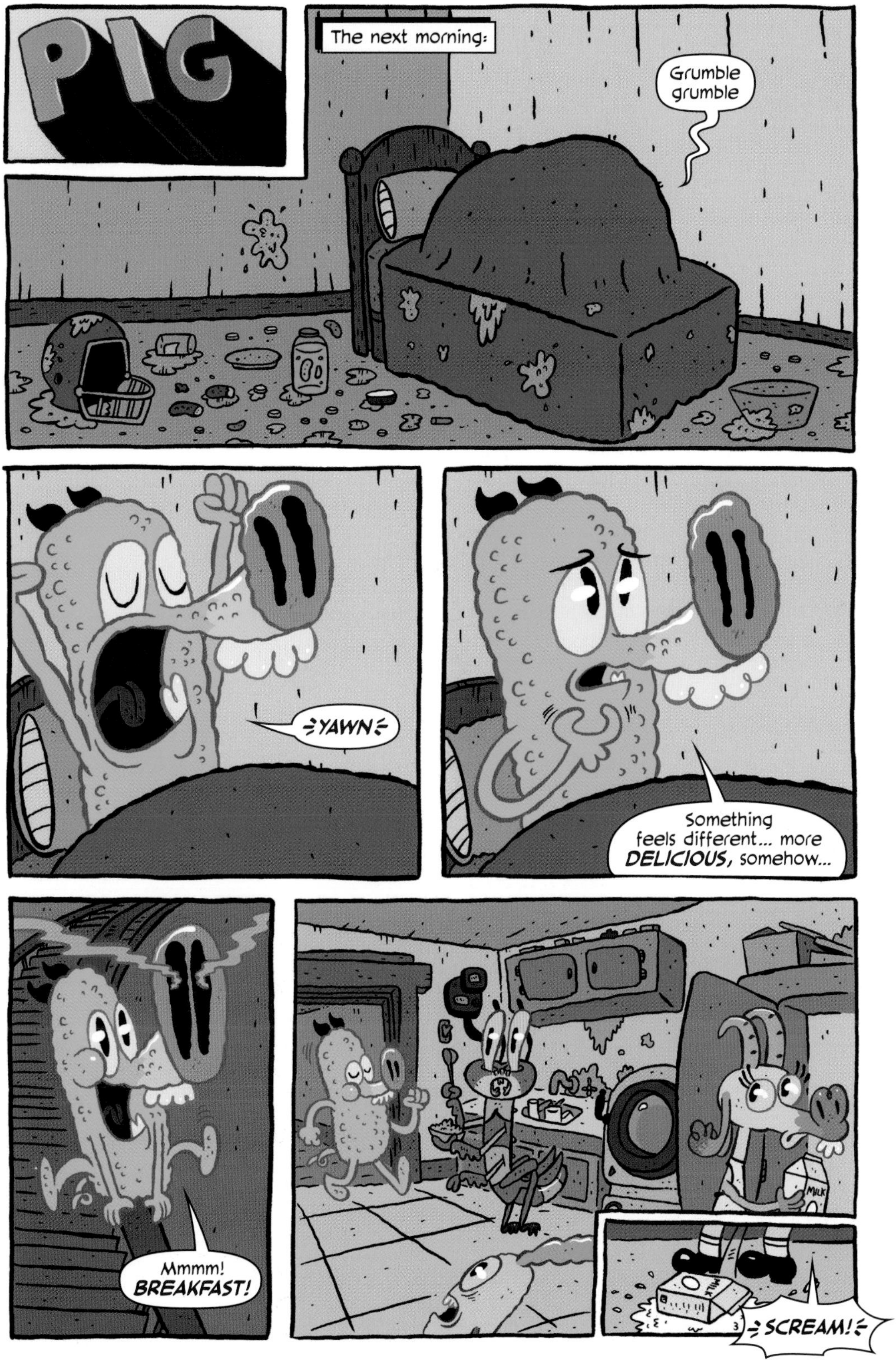
PIG
The next morning:
Grumble grumble
YAWN
Something feels different... more DELICIOUS, somehow...
Mmmm! BREAKFAST!
MILK
SCREAM!

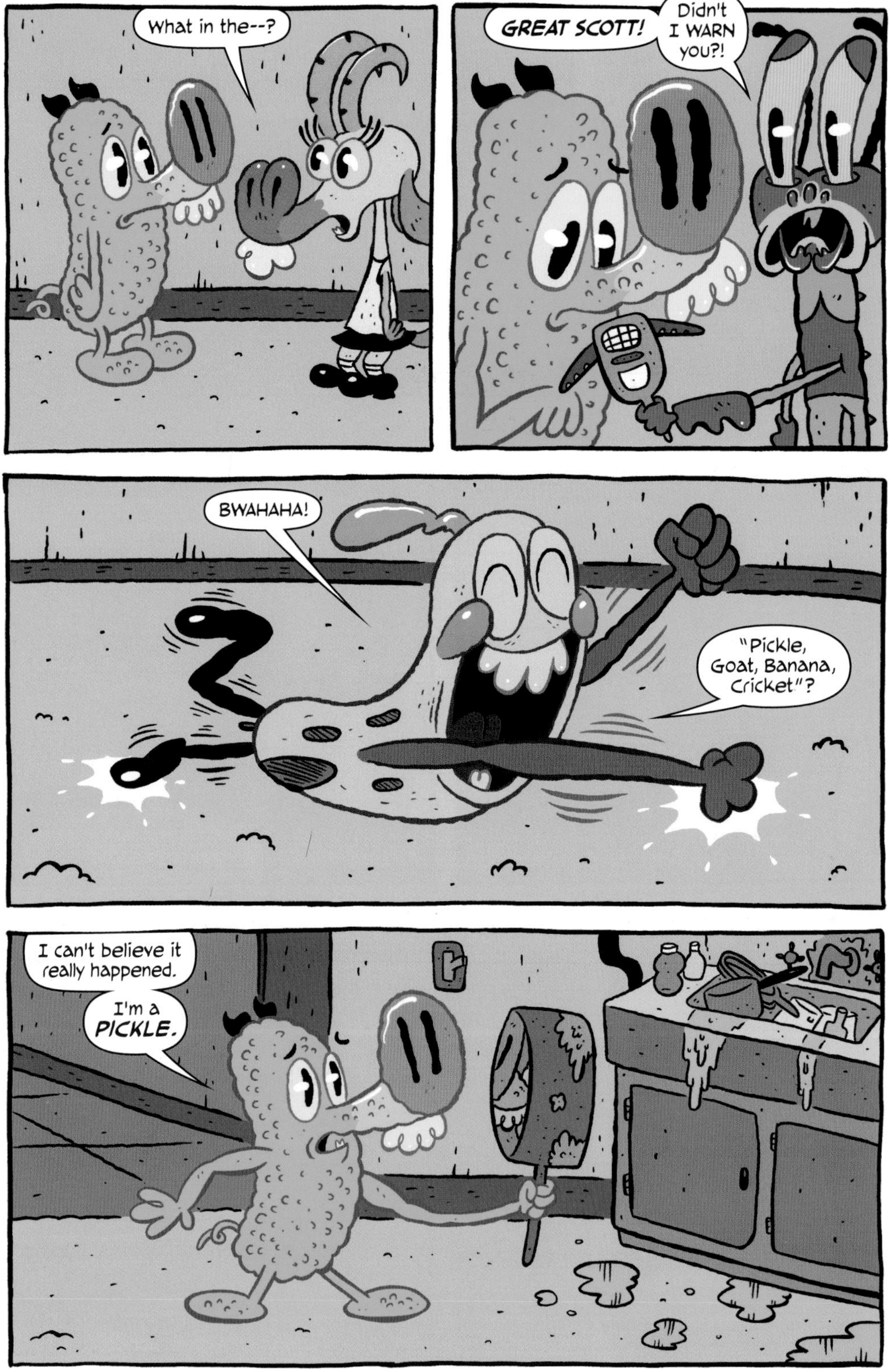
What in the--?
GREAT SCOTT!
Didn't I WARN you?!
BWAHAHA!
"Pickle, Goat, Banana, Cricket"?
I can't believe it really happened.
I'm a *PICKLE.*

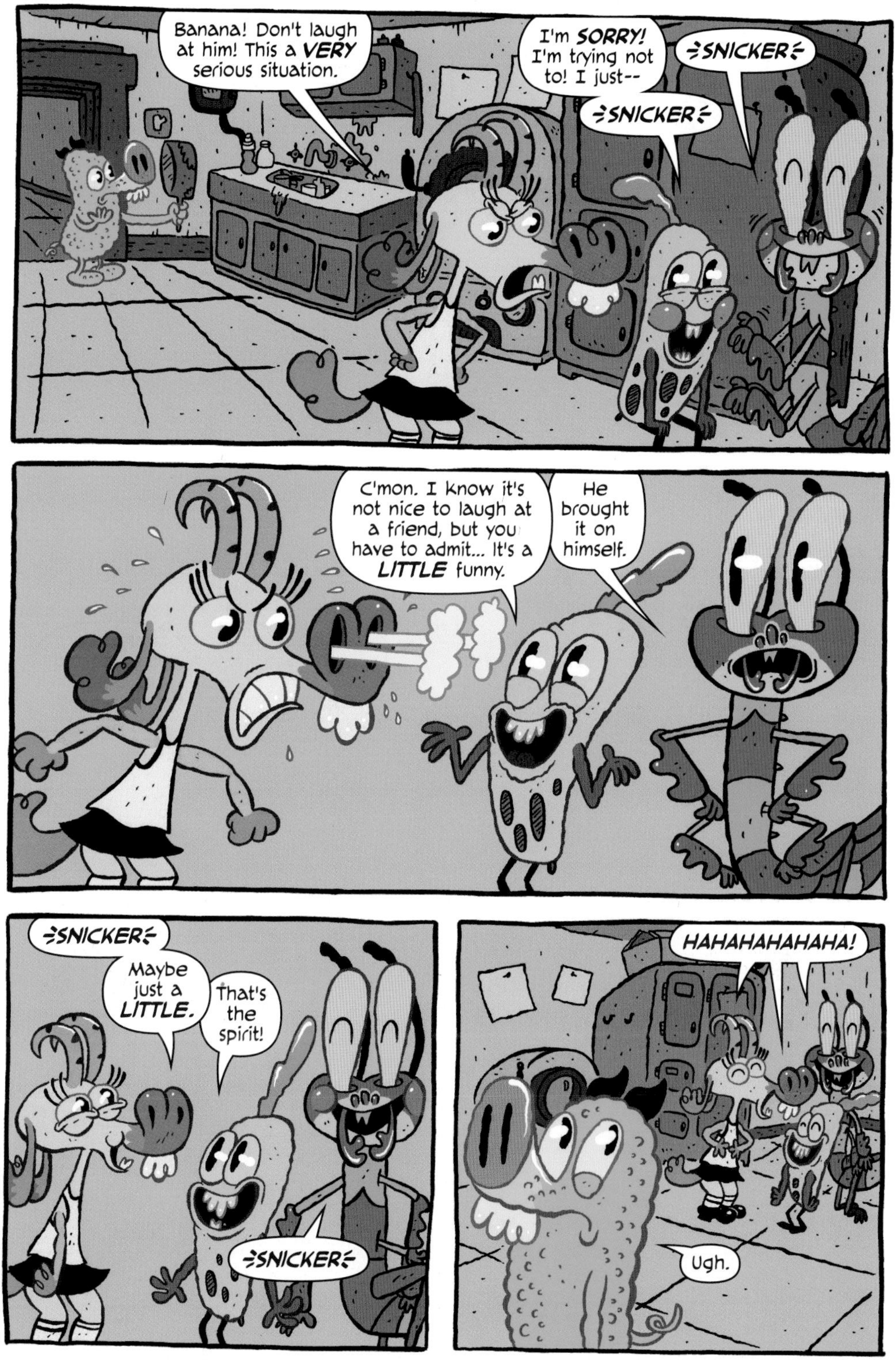
Banana! Don't laugh at him! This a VERY serious situation.
I'm SORRY! I'm trying not to! I just--
SNICKER
SNICKER
C'mon. I know it's not nice to laugh at a friend, but you have to admit... It's a LITTLE funny.
He brought it on himself.
SNICKER
Maybe just a LITTLE.
That's the spirit!
SNICKER
HAHAHAHAHAHA!
Ugh.

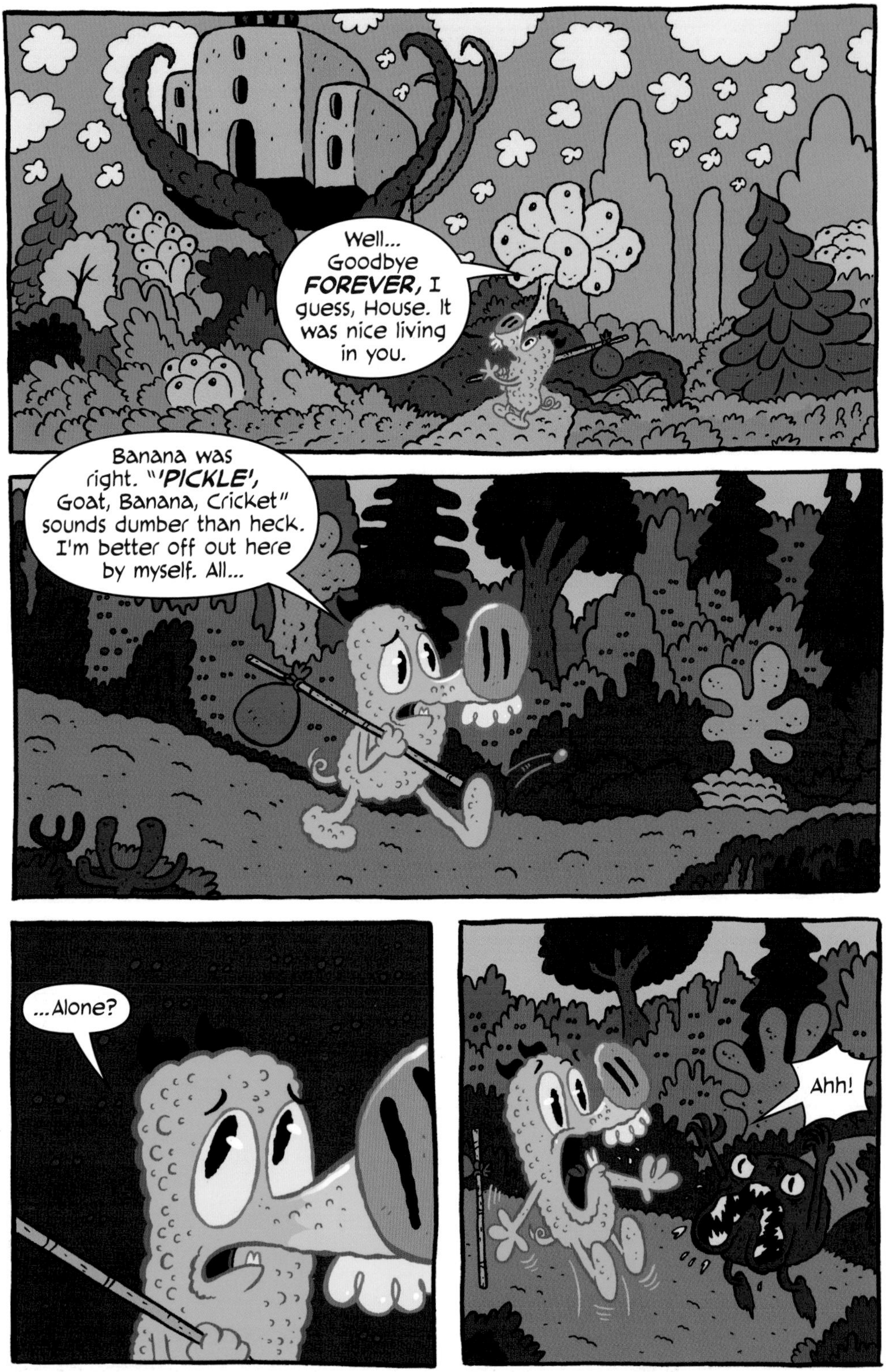
Well... Goodbye FOREVER, I guess, House. It was nice living in you.
Banana was right. "'PICKLE', Goat, Banana, Cricket" sounds dumber than heck. I'm better off out here by myself. All...
...Alone?
Ahh!

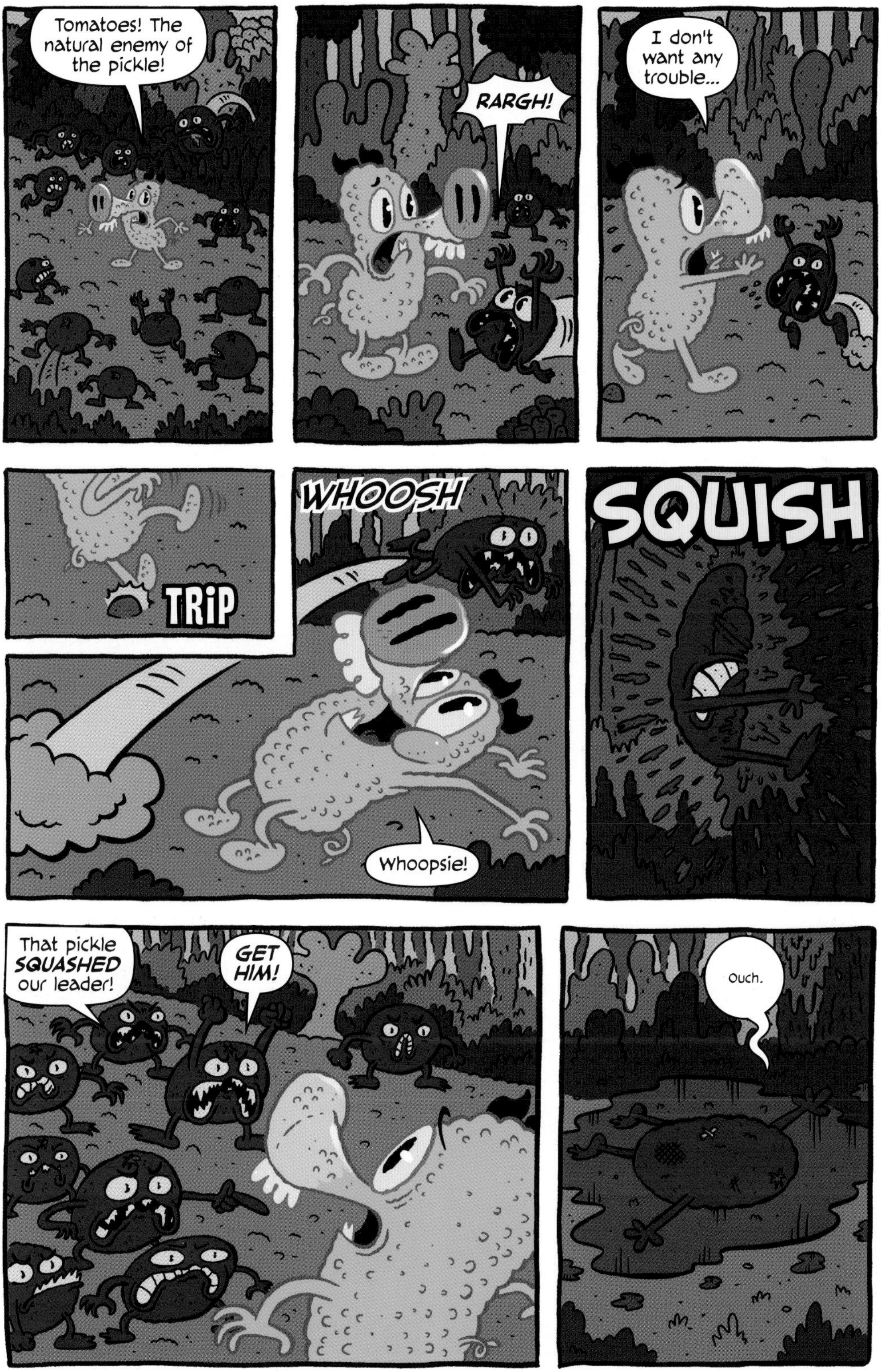
Tomatoes! The natural enemy of the pickle!
RARGH!
I don't want any trouble...
TRiP
WHOOSH
Whoopsie!
SQUISH
That pickle SQUASHED our leader!
GET HIM!
Ouch.

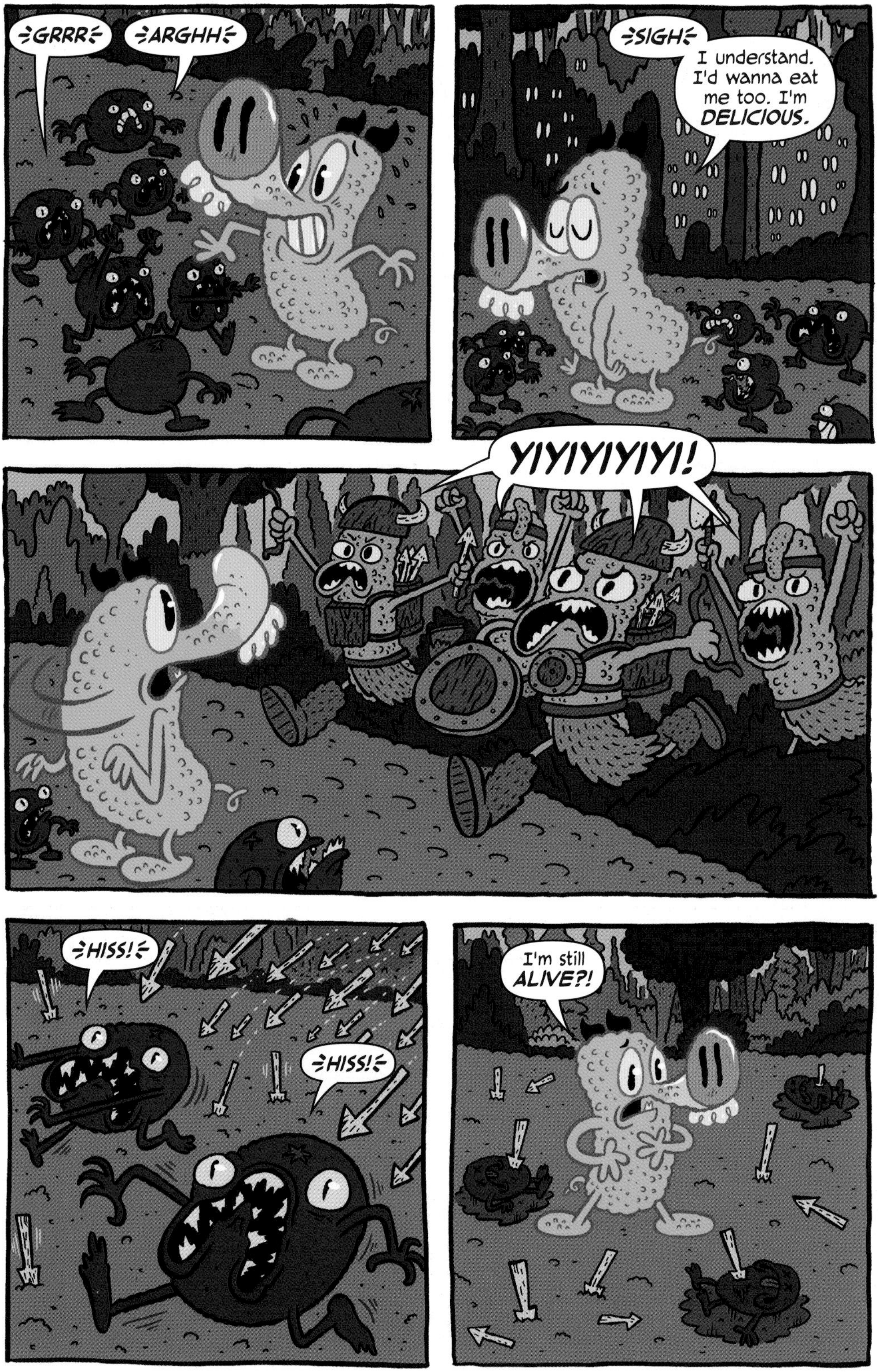
GRRR
ARGHH
SIGH
I understand. I'd wanna eat me too. I'm DELICIOUS.
YIYIYIYIYI!
HISS!
HISS!
I'm still ALIVE?!

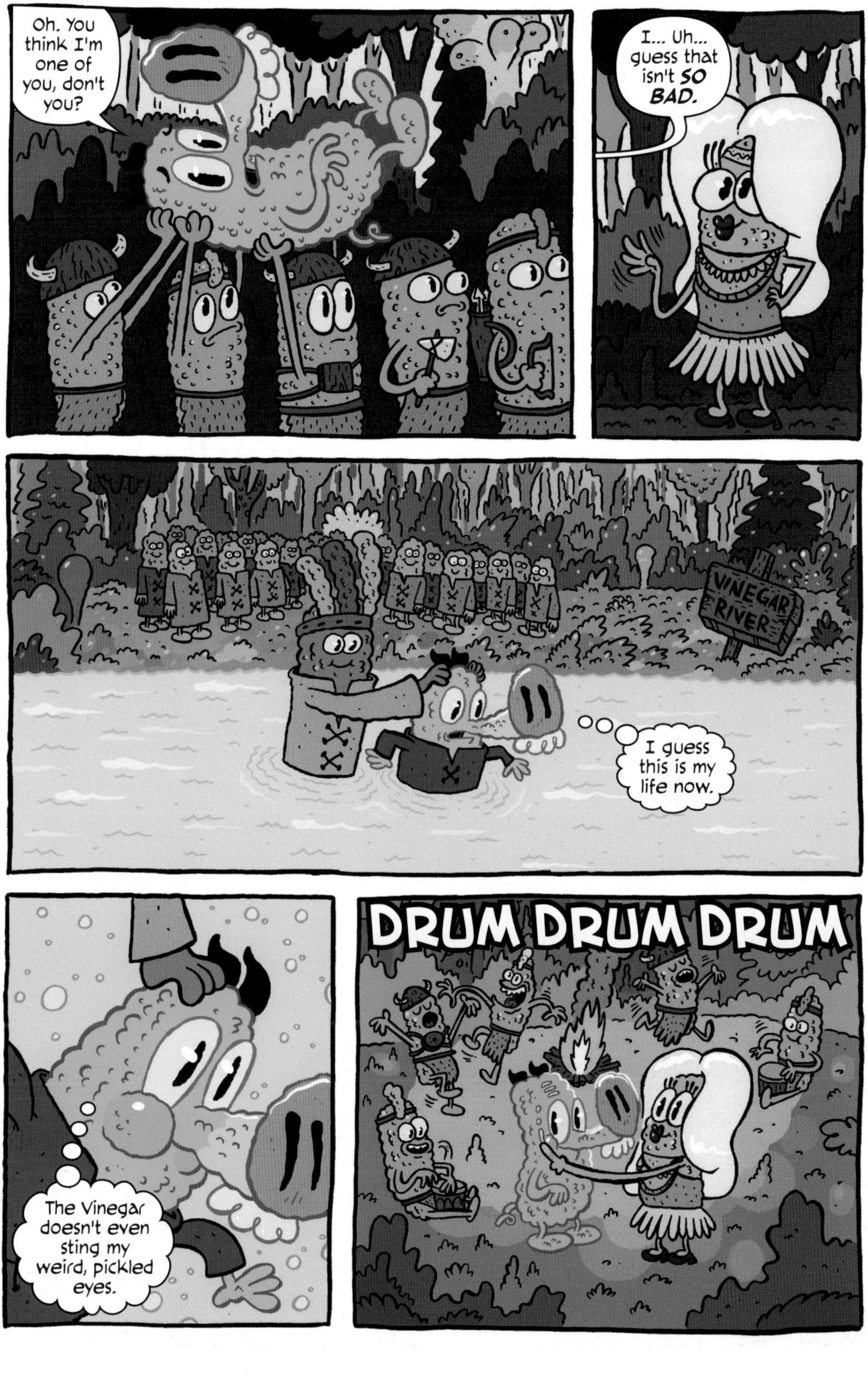
Oh. You think I'm one of you, don't you?
I... Uh... guess that isn't **SO BAD.**
VINEGAR RIVER
I guess this is my life now.
The Vinegar doesn't even sting my weird, pickled eyes.
DRUM DRUM DRUM

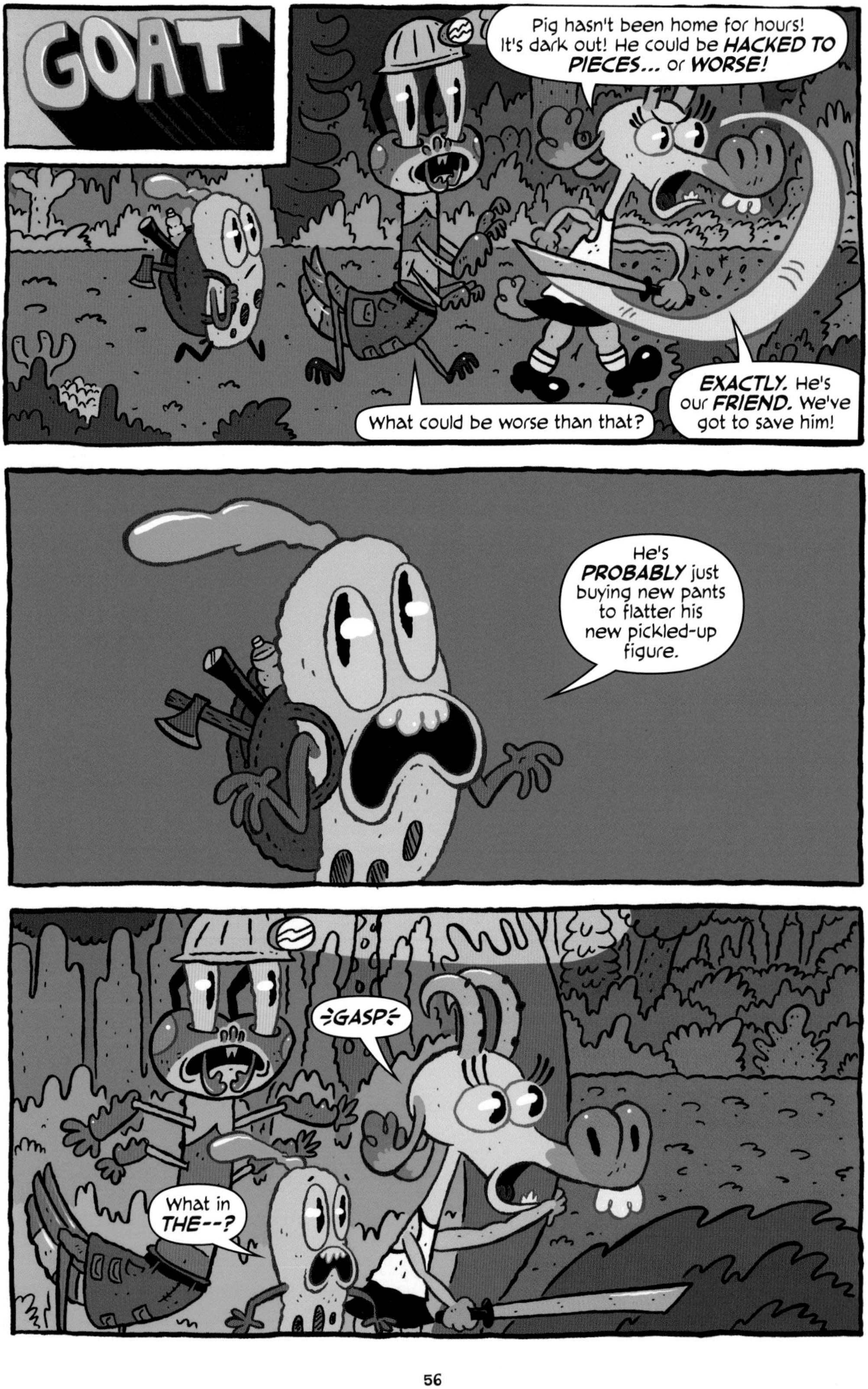
GOAT
Pig hasn't been home for hours! It's dark out! He could be HACKED TO PIECES... or WORSE!
What could be worse than that?
EXACTLY. He's our FRIEND. We've got to save him!
He's PROBABLY just buying new pants to flatter his new pickled-up figure.
GASP
What in THE--?

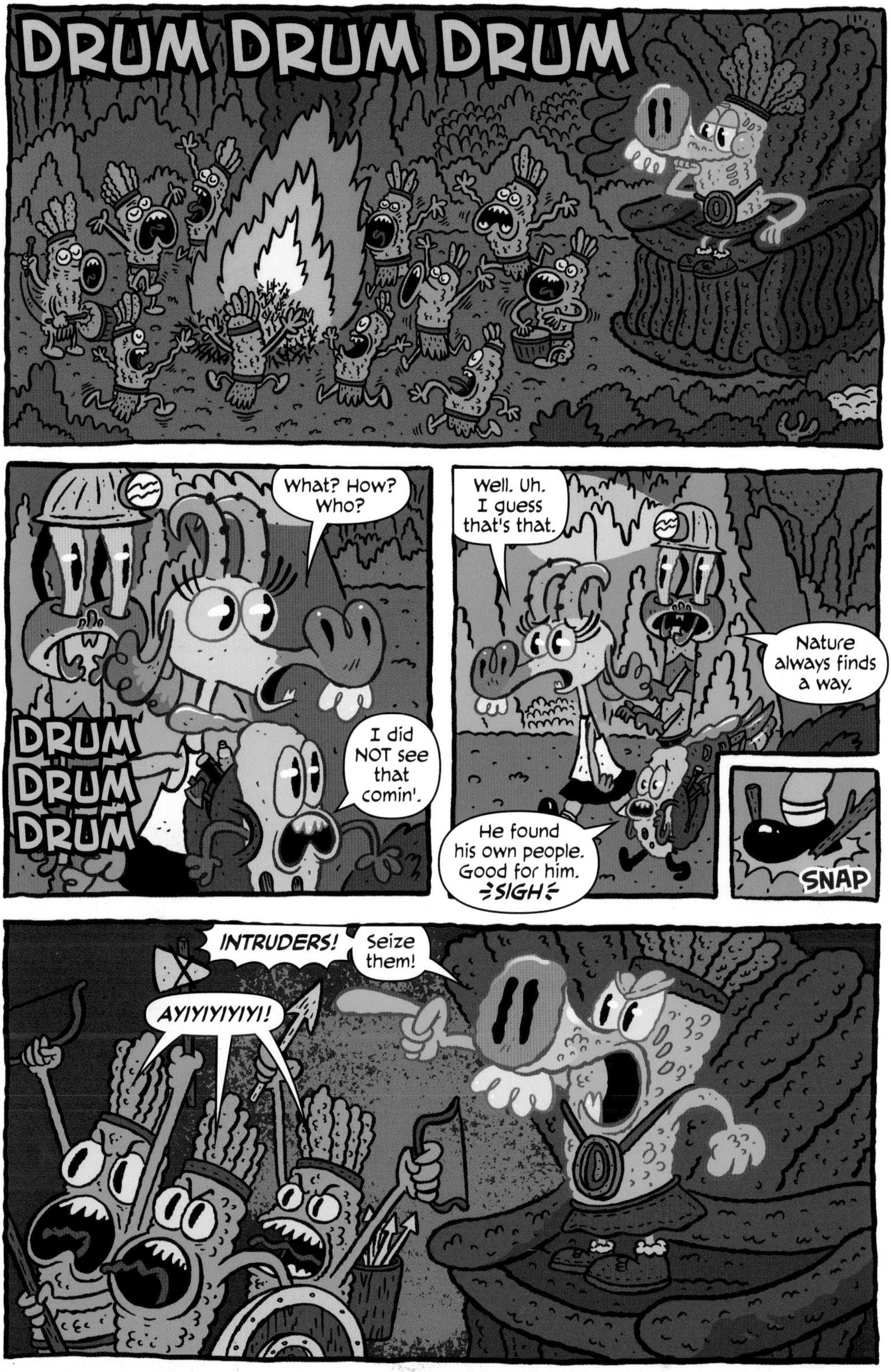
DRUM DRUM DRUM
What? How? Who?
DRUM DRUM DRUM
I did NOT see that comin'.
Well. Uh. I guess that's that.
Nature always finds a way.
He found his own people. Good for him. SIGH
SNAP
INTRUDERS!
Seize them!
AYIYIYIYIYI!

BANANA

I told you we shouldn't have brought so much **STUFF!**

I brought snacks in case we got hungry on our rescue mission. **SUE ME.**

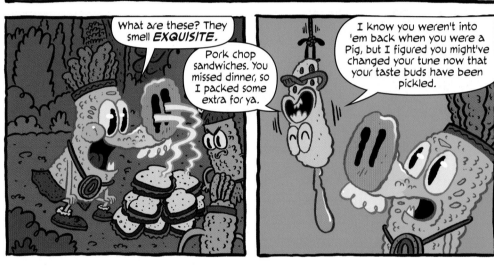

What are these? They smell **EXQUISITE.**

Pork chop sandwiches. You missed dinner, so I packed some extra for ya.

I know you weren't into 'em back when you were a Pig, but I figured you might've changed your tune now that your taste buds have been pickled.

SHRUG

SCARF

CHOMP

CHOMP

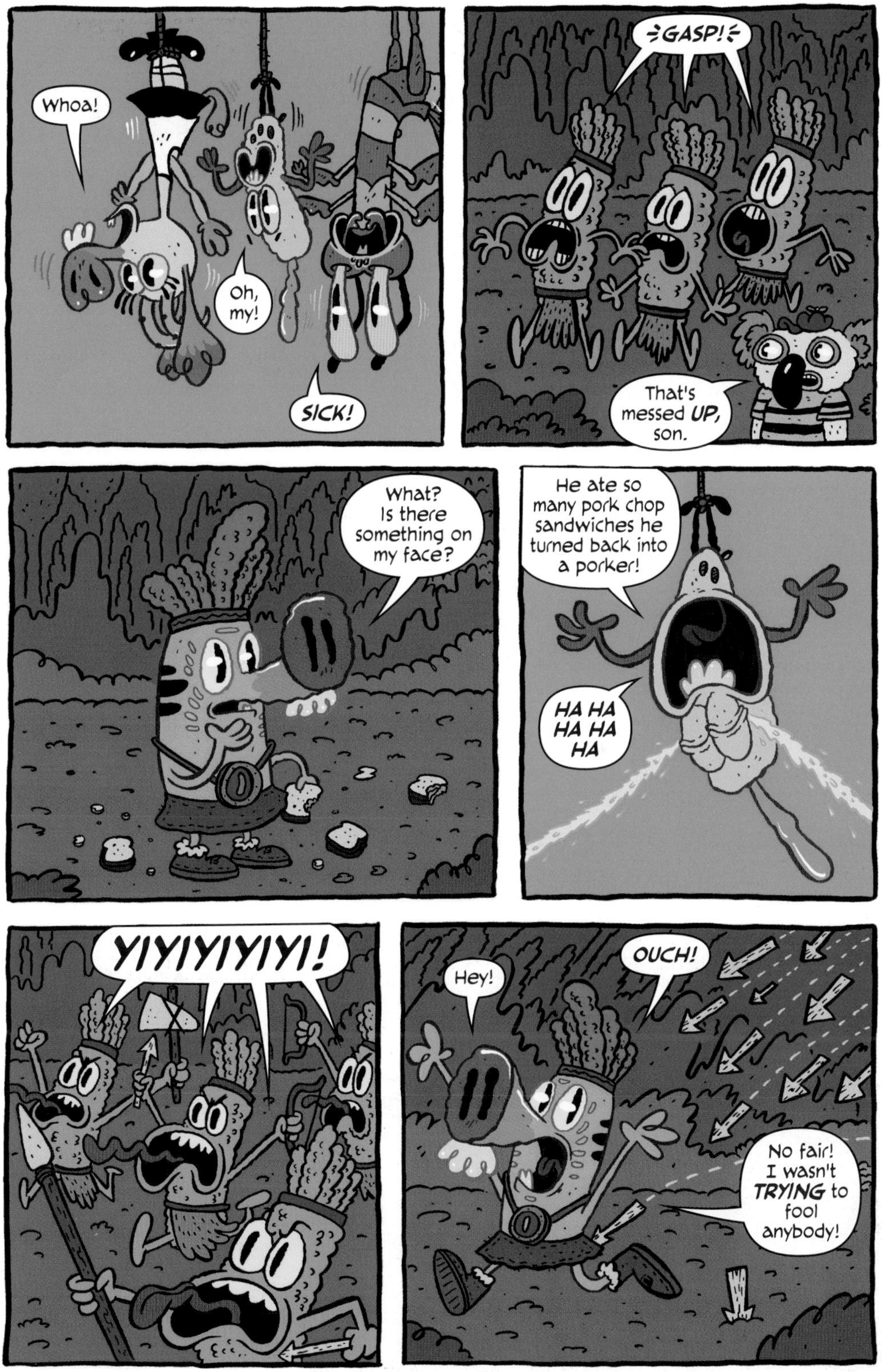
Whoa!
Oh, my!
SICK!
GASP!
That's messed UP, son.
What? Is there something on my face?
He ate so many pork chop sandwiches he turned back into a porker!
HA HA HA HA HA
YIYIYIYIYI!
Hey!
OUCH!
No fair! I wasn't TRYING to fool anybody!

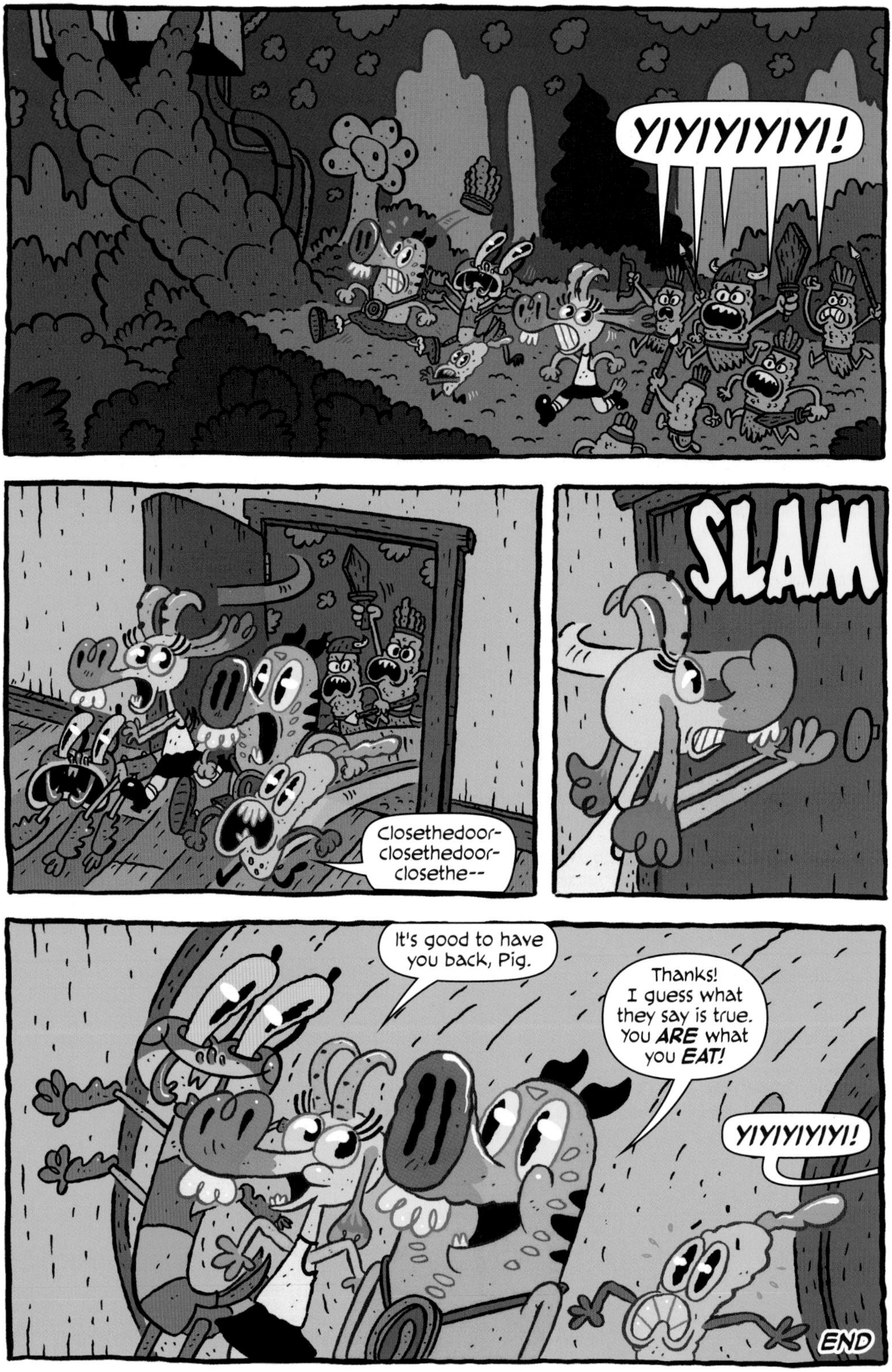
YIYIYIYIYI!
SLAM
Closethedoor-closethedoor-closethe--
It's good to have you back, Pig.
Thanks! I guess what they say is true. You **ARE** what you **EAT!**
YIYIYIYIYI!
END

WATCH OUT FOR PAPERCUTZ

Welcome to the frenetic, fast-paced, fun-filled, first PIG GOAT BANANA CRICKET graphic novel from Papercutz—those hard-working, semi-gluten-free comic-makers dedicated to publishing graphic novels for all ages. I'm Jim Salicrup, the pork-eating Editor-in-Chief, and I'm here to tell you a couple of interesting behind-the-scenes tales regarding how this graphic novel came to be! Let's start with how Papercutz and Nickelodeon came together. Sure, you might've heard this story before in the first SANJAY AND CRAIG, BREADWINNERS, and HARVEY BEAKS graphic novels, but like most legends, such tales are meant to be retold, so here we go again...

Over ten years ago, Papercutz publisher Terry Nantier and I founded this little comicbook company to address a need—there just didn't seem to be enough comics and graphic novels for kids. After ten years of producing all types of comics for all ages, we made an incredible deal with the awesome folks at Nickelodeon to create a line of graphic novels based on their latest and greatest new animated series. This really is a match made in cartoon heaven -- Nickelodeon, loved by millions of kids for their brilliant cartoon shows and characters, and Papercutz, the graphic novel publisher devoted to creating the best comics for kids—together at last!

Terry and I, along with Joan Hilty and Linda Lee, got to spend a day at the Nickelodeon Animation Studio where we talked about our plans with the creators of Sanjay and Craig, Breadwinners, and more. Everyone was excited and as thrilled as we were about the characters leaping off the TV screen and onto the comicbook page!

To kick off this historic publishing partnership, we launched an all-new NICKELODEON MAGAZINE, which in addition to features such as posters, activities, calendars, etc., is jam-packed with comics—the very same comics we'll be collecting in our graphic novels. The magazine is available wherever magazines are sold, and is also available as a subscription. Just go to Papercutz.com/nickmag for all the details.

Bethany Bryan (Editor/Papercutz) and Joan Hilty (Comics Editor/Nickelodeon) working with the writers and artists have come up with the PIG GOAT BANANA graphic novel you see before you. We hope you enjoy it as much as we do — after all, we did this all for you!

It's possible that someone out there is thinking, wait a minute, didn't I see this somewhere before? Yes, of course, all of the comics have already appeared in NICKELODEON MAGAZINE, as we mentioned, but "Crazy Photo Safari" was also published as a free mini-comic given away at Comic-Con International: San Diego by Nickelodeon and Papercutz to celebrate both the then-upcoming TV series and graphic novels. It's also possible, that someone with a really great memory, might even recall the May 2005 issue of NICKELODEON MAGAZINE, which featured a two-page comic featuring "a pig, a banana, a robot, and a toilet." Despite that comic being signed "by Hector Mumbly," it really was by — you guessed it!—Johnny Ryan and Dave Cooper, the creators of PIG GOAT BANANA CRICKET! Let's just say that this series has had an interesting creative journey, and that it's really cool that something that started as comics has come full circle back to being a comic again.

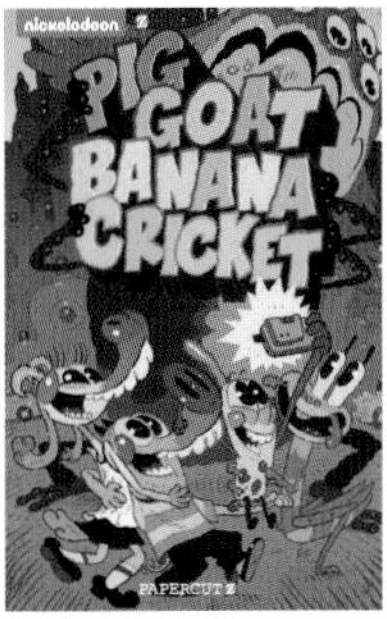
nickelodeon
PIG GOAT BANANA CRICKET
PAPERCUTZ
Mini Comic

And for those of you who remember the animated pilot which was called "Pig Goat Banana Mantis," we're sure that'll probably be the answer in an upcoming Trivia Quiz in NICKELODEON MAGAZINE!

But enough about the past! There's even more in store for you in the future! For example, in a few pages you'll even get to see a short preview of SANJAY AND CRAIG #3 "Story Time for Sanjay and Craig." But even more exciting is that PIG GOAT BANANA CRICKET will return in an all-new graphic novel series entitled NICKELODEON PANDEMONIUM, coming your way soon! Not only will it feature Pig Goat Banana Cricket, but don't be surprised if Sanjay and Craig, Breadwinners, and Harvey Beaks are included as well! In other words, the best is yet to come!

Thanks,

Jim

STAY IN TOUCH!

EMAIL:	salicrup@papercutz.com
WEB:	papercutz.com
TWITTER:	@papercutzgn
FACEBOOK:	PAPERCUTZGRAPHICNOVELS
FANMAIL:	Papercutz, 160 Broadway, Suite 700, East Wing, New York, NY 10038

A Special Preview of SANJAY & CRAIG #3 "Storytime with Sanjay and Craig"

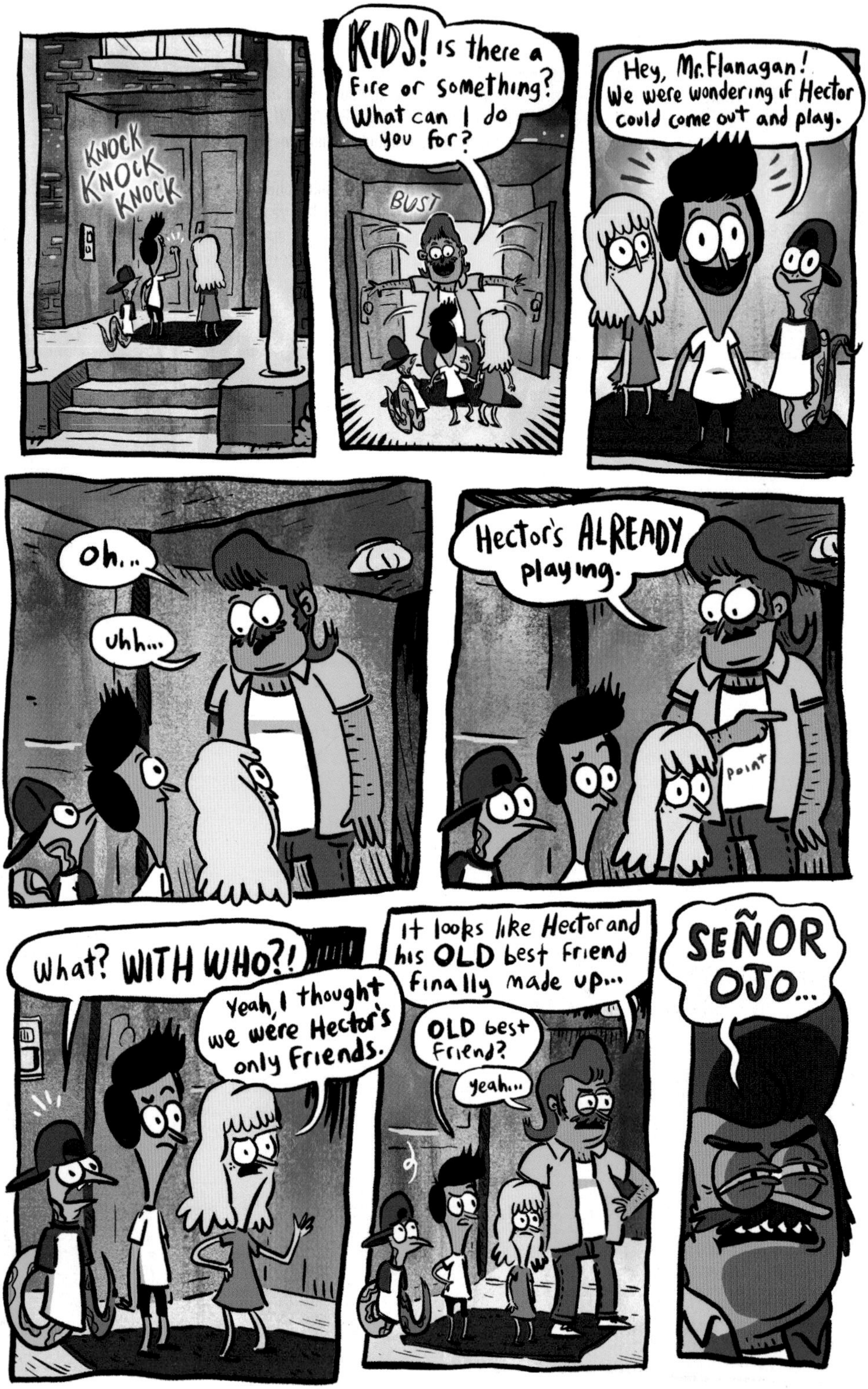
KNOCK KNOCK KNOCK
KIDS! is there a Fire or something? What can I do you for?
BUST
Hey, Mr. Flanagan! We were wondering if Hector could come out and play.
Oh...
uhh...
Hector's ALREADY playing.
point
What? WITH WHO?!
Yeah, I thought we were Hector's only Friends.
It looks like Hector and his OLD best friend finally made up...
OLD best Friend?
yeah...
SEÑOR OJO...

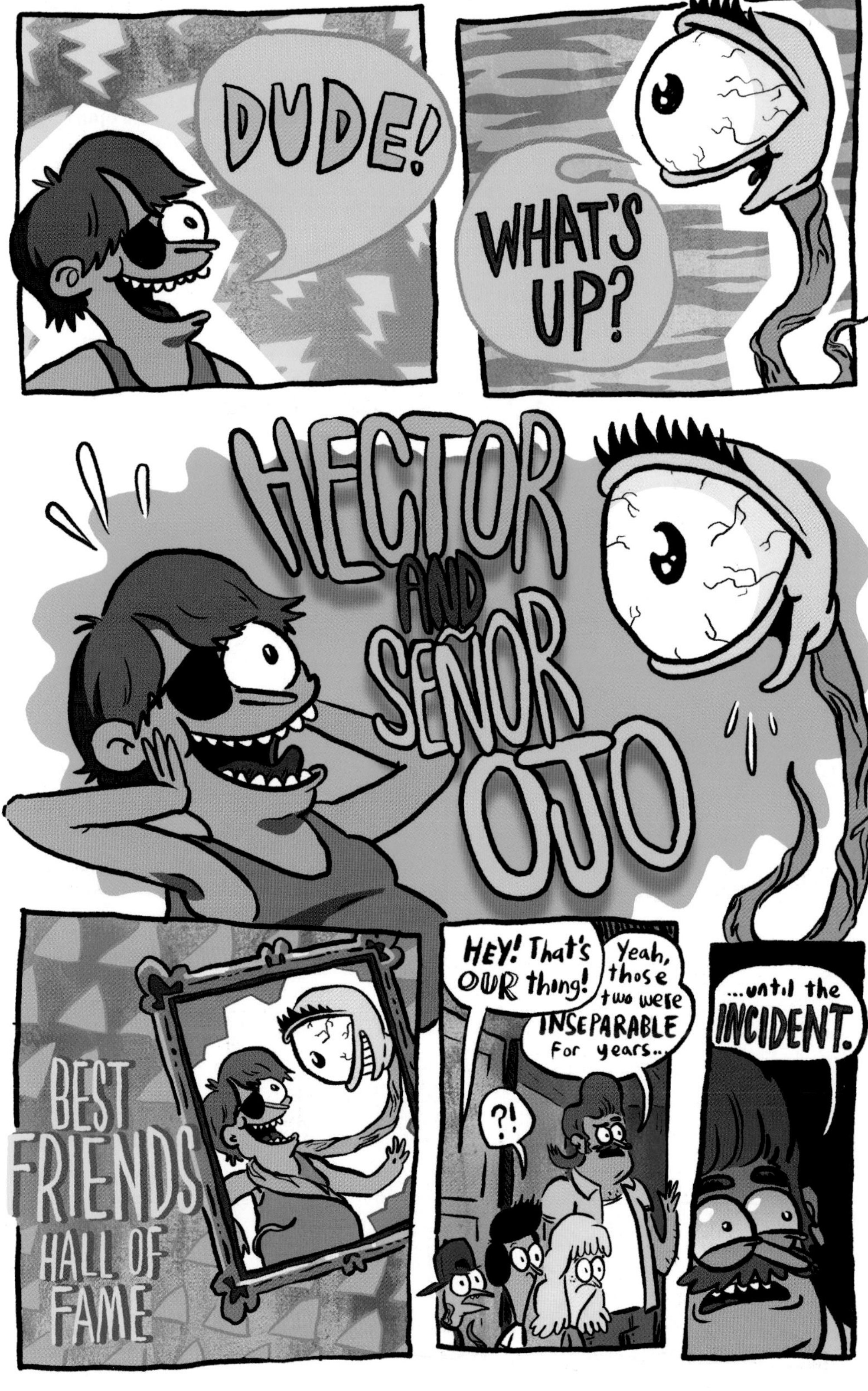
DUDE!
WHAT'S UP?
HECTOR AND SEÑOR OJO
BEST FRIENDS HALL OF FAME
HEY! That's OUR thing!
Yeah, those two were INSEPARABLE for years...
?!
...until the INCIDENT.

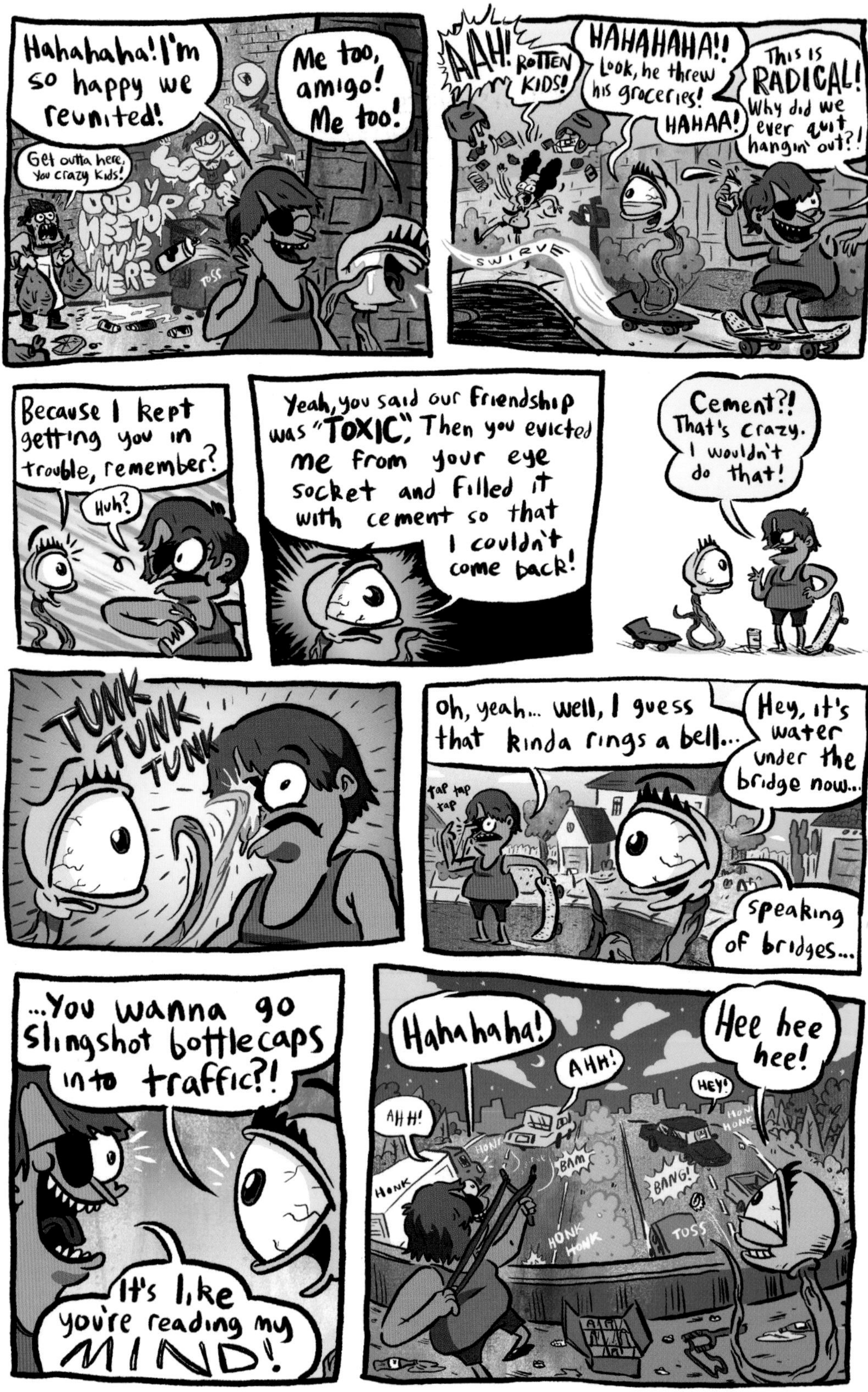

Hahahaha! I'm so happy we reunited!
Get outta here, you crazy kids!
Me too, amigo! Me too!
TOSS
AAH! ROTTEN KIDS!
HAHAHAHA!! Look, he threw his groceries! HAHAA!
This is RADICAL! Why did we ever quit hangin' out?!
SWIRVE
Because I kept getting you in trouble, remember?
Huh?
Yeah, you said our friendship was "TOXIC." Then you evicted me from your eye socket and filled it with cement so that I couldn't come back!
Cement?! That's crazy. I wouldn't do that!
TUNK TUNK TUNK
Oh, yeah... well, I guess that kinda rings a bell...
tap tap tap
Hey, it's water under the bridge now...
Speaking of bridges...
...You wanna go slingshot bottlecaps into traffic?!
It's like you're reading my MIND!
Hahahaha!
AHH!
AHH!
HEY!
Hee hee hee!
HONK
BAM
BANG!
HONK HONK
TOSS